MEET THE ~~FORTUNES~~ MENDOZAS!

Mendoza of the Month: Matteo Mendoza

Age: 28

Vital statistics: Brown bedroom eyes and a quiet soulfulness that could melt a lady's heart.

Claim to fame: So far, the Miami-born pilot has been flying under the radar. But not for long!

Romantic prospects: They'd be a lot better if his flirtatious brother Cisco wasn't around. The two of them always seem to be in competition— especially for the heart of gorgeous and elusive Rachel Robinson.

"To my brother, love is just a game. But for me, the stakes are much higher. I will fight for Rachel if I have to. She's the one I've been waiting for. So far, she's been holding back. Why? Could my radar be that far off? Is she really interested in Cisco? Or is there something else she could be hiding?"

**THE FORTUNES OF TEXAS:
COWBOY COUNTRY:
Lassoing Hearts from Across the Pond**

Dear Reader,

Welcome back to another chapter in the Fortune saga. The budding relationship between the two main characters is at the forefront of this story, yet both their families play strong supporting roles, not just in these two people's lives but in the way they react to one another, as well as the way they react to love.

Rachel Robinson left the comforts of her wealthy home five years ago, saying she wanted to "find herself." The truth was that she had accidentally stumbled across a family secret that shook the very foundations of her world. Here in Horseback Hollow, she is working part-time as a hostess at the Hollows Cantina, and has also taken on an internship at the newest branch of the Fortune Foundation, set to open in the following month.

She crosses paths with Matteo and Cisco Mendoza, in town for their sister's wedding. She finds herself instantly attracted to the sensitive, handsome younger Matteo, but his older brother asks her out first. Matteo and Cisco have been competing with one another since birth, but this is one prize Matteo is determined that his brother isn't going to win.

Drawn to Matteo, Rachel wonders if she can trust her own judgment since it went so wildly astray with her father. And if she follows her heart, will Matteo turn away once he knows about the secret she's hiding?

Come, read, find out. And (hopefully) be entertained while you do it.

As ever, I thank you for taking the time to read one of my books and from the bottom of my heart, I wish you someone to love who loves you back.

All the best,

Marie Ferrarella

Mendoza's Secret Fortune

Marie Ferrarella

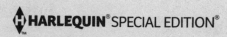

HARLEQUIN SPECIAL EDITION®

Special thanks and acknowledgment to Marie Ferrarella for her contribution to
The Fortunes of Texas: Cowboy Country continuity.

ISBN-13: 978-0-373-65871-8

Mendoza's Secret Fortune

Copyright © 2015 by Harlequin Books S.A.

Recycling programs for this product may not exist in your area.

Printed in U.S.A.

www.Harlequin.com

USA TODAY bestselling and RITA® Award-winning author **Marie Ferrarella** has written more than two hundred books for Harlequin, some under the name Marie Nicole. Her romances are beloved by fans worldwide. Visit her website, marieferrarella.com.

Books by Marie Ferrarella

Harlequin Special Edition

Matchmaking Mamas

Diamond in the Ruff
Dating for Two
Wish Upon a Matchmaker
Ten Years Later...
A Perfectly Imperfect Match
Once Upon a Matchmaker

The Fortunes of Texas: Welcome to Horseback Hollow

Lassoed by Fortune

The Fortunes of Texas: Southern Invasion

A Small Fortune

Montana Mavericks: Back in the Saddle

Real Vintage Maverick

Harlequin Romantic Suspense

Mission: Cavanaugh Baby
Cavanaugh on Duty
A Widow's Guilty Secret
Cavanaugh's Surrender
Cavanaugh Rules
Cavanaugh's Bodyguard

Visit the Author Profile page at Harlequin.com for more titles.

To
Marcia Book Adirim,
whose mind works on
many more levels
than mine does

Chapter One

"Hey, Rach. Nice to see you again!" the regular lunch customer at The Hollows Cantina called out as he walked into the dining area with several friends.

With a compliant smile, the hostess drew several menus into her hands and led the rather vocal men to table number four, listening to them as they swapped stories and laughed.

She was getting pretty good at this, Rachel Robinson silently congratulated herself, especially since nothing in her previous life could have prepared her for doing something like this. Back then, she'd been accustomed to being the one who was served, not the one doing the serving.

Poor little rich girl.

That was the title, Rachel thought, that probably would have best described her as little as five years ago, but not anymore. She had taken great pains to hide any hint of her past life. No one in this tiny, one-horse town nestled approximately four hundred miles away from Austin had any idea that she was one of Gerald Robinson's daughters. They had no clue that her father was a wealthy computer genius who had more than left his giant mark on the tech world.

Her father had left his mark in other places as well, places she'd learned about only when she had accidentally stumbled across the truth five years ago. Her discovery had prompted her sudden exodus to Horseback Hollow, a place she had found by closing her eyes and then jabbing her index finger at a map of Texas.

A place where she was hoping to get a completely new start and be herself rather than Gerald Robinson's daughter.

It seemed rather ironic to her to be here at this point in her life. She had already reinvented herself once. Her childhood had been spent mostly on the outside looking in.

Odd girl out, that was her.

She was always the tallest girl in her class, at times taller than all the boys, as well. Tall and thin as a rail, which made her an easy target for other girls who felt their own stock was enhanced if they could bring hers down by several notches.

So they did.

Though she had thought of herself as an outcast, her father, in one of his rare times at home rather than at work, insisted that she was "special." To that end, he saw to it that she was enrolled in a number of different classes—dance, tennis, piano, whatever it took—and Rachel discovered that she was good at all of them.

That discovery fueled her confidence, and Mother Nature stepped in to take care of the gawky, awkward issue. Thinking she was doomed to go through life all knobby knees and elbows, Rachel was delighted to find herself transforming from a plain duckling to a lovely swan.

It was a transformation that did *not* go unnoticed by the local males. Suddenly the center of attention, she continued to be so through her college years. She was flying high when her entire world came into question at the end of her senior year, courtesy of a former friend turned jealous rival. A rival who chose the dance floor at the senior-week dance to humiliate her by making certain allegations and so-called secret facts about her father public.

That was when Rachel's world came crashing down around her. A short time later, she arrived in Horseback Hollow.

Though done in haste, it had turned out not to be such a bad move after all. She didn't mind hard work. It brought her a sense of satisfaction. And here she wasn't anyone's daughter or sibling. She was just Rachel Robinson, hardworking restaurant hostess.

And she liked it that way, Rachel thought as she deposited the menus on the table, presenting each of the three men with the daily-special cards.

As she distributed them, she became acutely aware that one of the men was sizing her up closely. He leered at her. Rachel quickly looked away.

"Your server will be right with you, and let me know if there'll be anything else you need," she said, addressing the trio.

"Maybe you could get us some extra napkins for

these two to use when they stop drooling," the oldest man at the table suggested.

Rachel flashed an automatic smile and told him, "I'll see what I can do, sir."

She was about to head back to the hostess station up front when the one who had been eyeing her so closely said, "Don't rush off so fast." He caught her by the wrist. "Where have you been all my life, darlin'?"

The inner feistiness that she always tried to keep under wraps broke through. She heard herself answering, "Well, for the first half of it, I wasn't even born."

Rather than being put off because his friends laughed at her response, the man, still holding her wrist, said, "Lively. I like that in a woman."

With a hard tug, Rachel pulled her wrist free. "Pushy. I don't like that in a man," she replied sweetly.

The man who had asked for extra napkins laughed and said, "She sure got your number, Walt."

She certainly did, Rachel thought. And that number was a big zero.

Matteo Mendoza was running late. There were few things he hated more, but sometimes—like today—it just couldn't be helped. Still, he knew that his older brother, Cisco, would have some sort of asinine remark to toss his way. He braced himself for the onslaught.

Preoccupied, he passed by the table with the boisterous cowboys and heard the whole exchange play out. The young woman was certainly far too beautiful for the job she was doing, but that didn't mean she deserved to be treated with anything but respect.

Rather than look for his father's table, he approached this one first.

"Problem here?" Matteo asked, coming up behind the attractive hostess.

"Just havin' a little fun. Nothing serious," the man called Walt said, raising his hands to indicate that it was hands-off from now on as far as he was concerned.

"Thank you," Rachel said to the tall, dark and handsome knight in shining armor who had ridden up to defend her honor. She moved away from the rowdy cowboys' table. "But that wasn't really necessary. I can take care of myself."

Matteo inclined his head, as if to agree with the young woman. "Nobody said you couldn't," he replied.

With that, he moved farther into the dining area, scanning it to find where his father and brother were seated.

For the most part, when he joined his brother, Cisco, and his father for lunch at The Hollows Cantina, Matteo was thinking about going home. Home in both his and Cisco's case was Miami. Being here, in this little town with the improbable name of Horseback Hollow, was nothing short of an overwhelming culture shock.

Initially, he and Cisco had come to this slow-as-molasses, underdeveloped Texas town because their baby sister, Gabriella, had inexplicably fallen in love in Horseback Hollow.

Specifically, he and Cisco had come out here for Gabi's wedding to Jude Fortune Jones.

But the wedding had come and gone, and much to

Matteo's chagrin, he and Cisco were still here. Their father had prevailed upon them to stay a little longer—as a personal favor to him.

Orlando Mendoza had been the first of their immediate family to come out here from Miami. It wasn't a sense of wanderlust that had prompted the patriarch's relocation, but rather a feeling of urgency, a search for a purpose. Orlando was desperately trying to find a way to go on with his life after losing the love of his life, his wife, Luz.

A former air force pilot who had retired to care for his ailing spouse, Orlando found new purpose in his life when he came to Horseback Hollow. He joined Sawyer and Laurel Fortune in their fledgling venture, the Redmond Flight School, and also used his expertise to help operate the occasional charter service they ran.

It was while he was flying one of the planes—a plane, as it turned out, that had been intentionally tampered with—that he suffered a plane crash and had gotten seriously injured. The moment she got the news, Gabi had been quick to fly in from Miami in order to nurse him back to health.

As luck would have it, Gabi wound up nursing herself right into a love affair. Marriage turned out to be a by-product of that affair.

It was obvious to Matteo that Gabi, as well as his father, really liked this town and preferred it to Miami. His father had already tried subtly to talk Cisco as well as him into relocating to Horseback Hollow. Orlando made no secret of the fact that he wanted nothing more than to have his entire family living somewhere in proximity.

Although he loved and respected his father, Matteo couldn't see himself staying here indefinitely, much less living here.

"No offense, Dad, but this place is just too small, too mundane and too rural for my tastes." Snagging another tortilla chip, he popped it into his mouth and then continued, "It's like everything moves in slow motion around here. They even roll up the sidewalks at ten o'clock." He nursed his tall, cold glass of beer.

"Now, Matteo, you know you are exaggerating," Orlando chided him.

"There's no nightlife here," Matteo countered, "not to mention that there's just no excitement whatsoever in this town." He leaned over the table to get closer to his father. "I'm not like you, Dad. I'm young. I need excitement."

Orlando laughed the way a man might when he saw himself in his son's words. Everyone needed to take risks and behave foolishly, getting it out of their system when they were still young. He fully understood that. But he also had a father's desire to have his children learn from his mistakes so that they wouldn't repeat them.

"Oh, there's excitement here in this town, *hijo*," he assured Matteo. "Trust me, there is excitement. It's just of a different nature."

Matteo smiled just before he tilted back his glass again. Obviously he and his father had *very* different definitions of "excitement," and he could understand that. At sixty-one, his father had earned the right to kick back and take it easy, while he, a pilot like his father and twenty-eight to boot, wanted nothing less than to take on anything that life might want to throw at him. Doing so got his adrenaline going and made him feel alive. He'd always had a competitive streak, especially when it came to his brother. He and Cisco had been competing against one another for as long as either one of them could remember.

"Give this place a chance," Cisco said with the thousand-watt smile that all the women within a ten-mile radius always found to be nothing short of spellbinding. "I know I am."

Matteo looked at his jet-setting older brother in disbelief. He'd been right. Cisco *had* decided to stay on for a while. He couldn't help wondering why. Cisco loved the pace in Miami as much as he did.

"You're staying?" he asked. There had to be an angle that Cisco was playing, but what?

Cisco lifted his glass in a mock toast to his brother, then drained it before answering, "That's what I just said."

Cisco liked to party more than he did. His choosing to stay here didn't make an iota of sense. "Why?" Matteo asked.

Cisco raised his broad shoulders and let them fall again in a vague, careless shrug. "Dad and Gabi seem sold on Horseback Hollow. That means there's got to be some merit to this town, right? I intend to stick around awhile and find out if I see it for myself. Might be some good real-estate investments going begging here." And then Cisco all but lit up. "Speaking of merit," he said, his attention directed toward something—or someone—he saw over his brother's head.

Curious, Matteo turned around in his chair, looking behind him. Which was when he saw her. The hostess he had verbally defended against the clowns at the other table a few minutes ago. She was heading their way. Matteo caught himself sitting up a little straighter.

When he had come to her assistance, he'd noted her height and the color of her long hair. He had of course observed that she was very attractive, but hadn't gone out of his way to really take in each aspect of her beauty. Besides, her looks had nothing to do with his coming to her defense, and his attention had been focused more on the men annoying her, anyway.

He could see her head-on now. Suddenly everything that had previously been on his mind evaporated from his brain. Matteo forgot all about missing Miami or being stuck in what he'd thought of as a one-horse town.

Forgot about everything except what was right there in front of him and coming closer.

Heaven in an apron.

He could almost feel the electrical charge this beautiful young woman seemed to radiate with every step she took.

Matteo had to remind himself to continue breathing. Air kept getting stuck in his lungs. And if his mouth were any dryer, dust would have come spilling out the second he tried to talk.

He wasn't the only one who was mesmerized by this vision. Out of the corner of his eye, Matteo saw that Cisco suddenly sat up, snapping to attention, his laid-back attitude becoming not quite so laid-back the second the hostess came into his line of vision.

As if on cue, the hostess stopped at their table, smiled and introduced herself to the trio.

"Hello, my name is Rachel, and I'll be your server

this afternoon. One of our regulars called in sick, and I'm covering for her." She glanced from Orlando to his two sons. Recognizing the one on the older man's right as the man who had come to her defense just a few minutes earlier, her smile grew wider in acknowledgment—chivalry should always be applauded. "Have you gentlemen decided yet?"

Matteo knew what he would have liked to order. *Her.* He kept that response to himself.

After his father and Cisco had placed their orders with the dark-haired, blue-eyed beauty, Matteo knew that he had ordered something, but for the life of him, he couldn't remember what less than three seconds after the words had left his mouth.

He had been fixated on the way her lips moved as she spoke and the way his entire system reacted to the melodic sound of her voice.

"Are you all right, Matteo?" his father asked once Rachel had retreated to the kitchen.

Cisco smirked. Annoyance flared in Matteo's veins. Now what?

"Yeah, sure. I'm fine, Dad." He turned to look at his father, puzzled. "Why would you ask that?"

"Well, I have known you for your whole life, and in all those years, I do not remember a single time when I saw you eating a salad as your main course. I believe you referred to salads as—"

"Cow food," Cisco interjected, unable to remain silent any longer. His laugh was full-bodied and hearty. And, right now, very annoying to Matteo. "I think my little brother was mesmerized by the lovely Rachel and didn't know what he was ordering, Dad."

"I wasn't mesmerized," Matteo protested with indignation, giving his brother a dirty look.

Matteo loved his older brother, but he hated being teased by Cisco. Cisco could be relentless, picking at him for days on end about a single thing if the spirit so moved him.

Now he grinned that wicked grin of his. "Hey, brother, I thought that she was a really hot little number, too."

Orlando could see that this had the makings of another family fight. Matteo sounded as if he was taking offense for the young woman—who surely hadn't a clue that she was the subject of this discussion, the older man surmised. As for Cisco, Orlando knew that the older boy loved to get Matteo riled up.

"We are all agreed that she is a very attractive young lady, Cisco. There is no reason for a dispute— or for you to give your brother a hard time," Orlando chided his older son.

Matteo frowned. He knew his father meant well, but he didn't need him coming to his aid this way. He wasn't ten years old and unable to hold his own against Cisco. Even at ten, he hadn't welcomed the interference.

"It's okay, Dad," Matteo said evenly, shifting his eyes to his brother. "Cisco didn't mean anything by that."

"Actually, I did," Cisco contradicted him. "Are you declaring dibs on Rachel? 'Cause if you are, it looks like maybe you've found that reason to hang around Horseback Hollow for a while—until she rebuffs you in favor of someone else, of course." Matteo's brother chuckled to himself as he continued eating the triangular chips from the bowl in the center of the table.

"You mean you?" The question came spontaneously to Matteo's lips, without any real thought necessary on his part.

Cisco's grin spread wider, annoying Matteo almost beyond words. "Just possibly."

"Matteo, Cisco," Orlando chided them sharply. "You're not children anymore, bent on competing until one of you collapses in exhaustion," he said. "It is time for you to behave like men."

"Men compete, Dad," Cisco reminded his father in all sincerity. "You know that."

For a moment, Orlando was catapulted back in time. He remembered his late wife, vividly remembered what he had gone through in order to win her hand in marriage. Remembered, too, what it had ultimately personally cost him.

"Sometimes men compete," Orlando admitted, then added, "but not my sons." He made the four words sound like an edict. "They do *not* compete against one another."

"Don't worry, Dad," Cisco assured him with a well-intentioned smile on his face. "It's not really a contest, is it, Matteo?" It wasn't so much a question as it was, in Cisco's opinion, a statement of fact. He raised his eyes to his brother's, waiting for a response. Or more accurately, waiting for his agreement.

Matteo knew just what his brother was inferring. That Matteo didn't stand a chance at winning over the striking young hostess, because Cisco had always been the lucky one when it came to all of their bets. More important, the one who always got the girl because he was so outgoing, charming and downright irresistible.

But Cisco was also the one whose relationships did not last, not even as long as the life cycle of a rose.

Terminating those relationships was always of his brother's own choosing, but that didn't change the fact that when all was said and done, Cisco wound up standing alone.

"She's a person, not property," Matteo pointed out tersely.

Cisco remained undaunted. "I completely agree," he replied in an even tone. He leaned forward just a touch. "So, tell the truth, brother. Does the lovely Rachel make you rethink leaving this tiny town?"

"She makes me rethink having you for a brother," Matteo informed him in as level a voice as he could manage. He was fighting the urge to cut Cisco down to size, but he had a feeling Cisco was looking forward to just that—so he refrained from playing into his brother's hands.

"Boys, *bastante*," Orlando declared, calling an end to the discussion before it got completely out of hand. "No fighting," he emphasized. "I asked you both here for a nice, peaceful lunch. I thought this restaurant might remind you a little of the ones you liked to go to back ho—back in Miami."

At the last moment, Orlando corrected himself. Referring to Miami as "home" was counterproductive to what he was currently attempting to promote— a sense that this place, Horseback Hollow, with its peaceful surroundings and room for growth, held a great deal of potential. Potential he felt that someone like Matteo—more so than Cisco—could tap into.

His youngest son was a pilot, like he was, but while he had been a risk-taker in his youth, Matteo admittedly was turning out to be far steadier at this point in his life than Orlando had been when *he* was twenty-eight.

Losing Luz just reinforced for Orlando that life was fleeting. However many years—or months—he had left, he wanted to spend them with his children. But at the same time, he knew that strong-arming them was not the way to proceed successfully.

Cisco—for the time being—was a done deal. He was staying in Horseback Hollow—he had even rented a small ranch house just outside of town. And of course, Gabi had already settled in here. Matteo, however, was going to require some major—and just possibly underhanded—convincing in order to get him to stick around. When they had come to eat at this restaurant, Orlando had thought his dilemma of winning his youngest son over was all but insurmountable.

Now, however, he finally had some hope. Many a man had done some unpredictable things in order to impress a young woman, and from what he could see, Matteo seemed to be pretty taken with that attractive hostess.

Orlando kept the conversation flowing, talking up the merits of Horseback Hollow, the closeness of its local citizens and how living here made a man focus on what was really important in life: his family and his health.

In recent months, the patriarch had regained the latter and was in the process of reinstituting the former.

With just a little luck and a healthy dose of his persuasion, Orlando felt he would succeed here, as well.

When the hostess returned shortly with their orders, Orlando carefully observed his younger son's reaction to her. That made him feel this indeed was the right path for him to concentrate on. His youngest son all but lit up like the proverbial Christmas tree when the woman approached.

Orlando noted that his older son seemed to come to life a little more, as well.

This had all the earmarks of an intense rivalry, Orlando observed. He had always tried to discourage that sort of thing, thinking that brothers should support one another, not attempt to best each other at every turn—especially when Cisco usually triumphed over Matteo. The last thing he wanted was for the latter to suffer another loss at the hands of his brother, but at this point, he couldn't think of another way to get Matteo to consider remaining in Horseback Hollow for a little while longer— and ideally, permanently—than bringing his son together with this hostess.

His secret hope was that if Matteo—and Cisco— did remain here for a number of weeks, both would be won over by the town's charm, and they would come to see that the merits of living in a small town trumped living in a large, indifferent metropolis where people lived next door to one another and remained strangers.

"Senorita, please, another round of cervezas for all of us," Orlando said once their server had emptied the tray she had carried to their table.

"Coming right up. And I'll bring back another bowl

of tortilla chips, as well," Rachel promised, picking up the empty woven basket and placing it on her tray. "Anything else?" she asked, her eyes sweeping over the three men.

"Maybe later," Cisco replied.

Rachel smiled as she inclined her head. "Later, then," she agreed cheerfully. "Anything else for you gentlemen?" she wanted to know, glancing at the other two men at the table.

Matteo stared down at what was to be his lunch. He honestly couldn't remember asking for the salad. In any event, that was *not* going to satisfy his appetite. "Yes. I'd like a cheeseburger, please," he said.

"Is something wrong with your salad?" she asked.

"No, I just thought that the cheeseburger would be more filling," Matteo explained, feeling as if he was tripping over his own tongue. He had never had Cisco's glib ability to spout clever rhetoric at the drop of a hat.

"Then you'd like me to take the salad back?" she asked.

"Not if it gets you into trouble." Now, why had he said something so stupid? Matteo upbraided himself. He should have just said yes and left it at that.

But to his relief, she smiled. "That's very considerate of you, but no, it won't." Picking up the salad, she placed it on her tray. "One cheeseburger, another round of cervezas and a bowl of chips coming up," she told him.

Captivated, Matteo watched her hips sway ever so slightly as she walked away from their table.

He could have sworn his body temperature went up a full five degrees.

Maybe more.

Chapter Two

Orlando looked at his youngest son and chuckled knowingly. "Well, I'm guessing there's at least one thing the Cantina has to offer that will have you coming back here again."

"Don't count on it." Cisco cavalierly waved away his father's words to his brother. "Matteo doesn't know a good thing when he sees it. I, on the other hand, can spot a good thing a mile away." Cisco leaned back in his chair, tilting it on its rear legs in order to get a better view of Rachel as she rounded a corner and disappeared into the kitchen.

"She's not a 'thing.' She's a woman," Matteo snapped at his brother. He didn't care for the way that Cisco had reduced the woman to the level of a mere object rather than giving her the proper due as a person.

"She certainly is that," Cisco agreed with a wide, appreciative and yet very devilish grin.

"No," Orlando announced firmly, instantly commanding his sons' attention.

"No, what?" Cisco asked as he looked at his father. They hadn't said anything that required a yes-or-no decision.

Orlando frowned, turning his affable face into a stern, somber mask. "No, you two are not going to butt heads and who knows what else while competing for the same woman."

Among Cisco's many talents was the ability to look completely innocent even when he was completely guilty. He assumed that look now as he turned his gaze on his father.

"What makes you think that Matteo and I are going to compete for the same woman, Dad?"

An exasperated look flashed across the patriarch's face. He was not about to be hoodwinked—or buried beneath his silver-tongued son's rhetoric.

"Is the Pope Catholic?" Orlando asked.

"Last time I checked," Cisco replied. His tone was respectful. The gleam in his eye, however, gave him away.

Orlando shook his head firmly. "And there you have your answer," he told Cisco. "I never said very much when you boys were growing up and insisted on turning everything into an emotional tug-of-war. I even thought—God forgive me—that it might help you two to build your character—"

"Matteo's a character all right," Cisco joked. "However, as far as I'm concerned—" He got no further.

Orlando looked as if his patience was wearing thin

and might even be in danger of giving way entirely. "But above all, I want you two to remember that you are brothers. No prize is worth sacrificing that relationship. Not even a woman you might think you love."

But he, Orlando added silently, was the exception that proved the rule. However, that wasn't something he was about to share with his sons. It went against the point he was trying to make.

"Don't worry, Dad. There isn't going to be any competition," Cisco assured his father as he slanted a quick glance at his brother.

Orlando nodded his silver head. "That's good to hear."

"By the way she looked at me, I've already won," Cisco concluded with that smile that always managed to get right under Matteo's skin.

And his brother knew it, Matteo thought, unable to do anything about it without getting on his father's bad side.

But he had to say *something*, however innocuous. So he did. "In your dreams," Matteo retorted.

"I agree with you there, Mattie. That little lady certainly is the stuff that dreams are made of," Cisco told his brother. "Besides, what difference does it make to you? Aren't you the one dying to leave this place in the dust and take off for good ol' Miami?"

Although when push came to shove—and under duress—Matteo would admit that he did love his brother, there were times when he would have liked nothing better than to strangle his irritating sibling with his bare hands.

Cisco had a way of getting to him like nobody

else could. So much so that if Cisco said "black," it instantly made him want to shout "white!"

Because of that feeling, it came as not much of a surprise to him when Matteo heard himself say, "Maybe I've changed my mind. Maybe I've decided to stick around Horseback Hollow for a little while longer."

Delighted and confident that given enough time here, he would be able to convince Matteo of the merits of living in this wonderful small town, Orlando leaned over and clapped his youngest son on the back. "That is wonderful news, my boy. Wonderful."

Matteo almost felt guilty about his father's reaction. He wasn't staying here because of his father. He was going to be hanging around a few extra days or so to see if he could win over the hostess before she succumbed to his sweet-talking brother.

"Yes, well, someone has to protect Horseback Hollow's unsuspecting women from the likes of him," Matteo told his father, nodding at his brother.

"And you've elected yourself that protector?" Cisco hooted, amusement highlighting his face at his brother's declaration. "That's one mighty tall order, little brother."

"Don't call me that, Cisco. I'm not your little brother," Matteo told him.

Cisco's amusement only grew. "Well, you're certainly not my big brother, now, are you, Mattie? I *am* the older one."

Matteo scowled. "Two years isn't all that much," he reminded his brother. And not even a full two years at that, Matteo thought.

"Oh, but it can amount to a lifetime under the right

set of circumstances," Cisco countered with a very mysterious grin that *really* annoyed Matteo.

Orlando sighed. He had had just about enough. Listening to this back-and-forth banter and bickering required something stronger to drink than just beer, but it was still too early in the day to contemplate downing any hard liquor.

"Might I remind you two boys that you no longer *are* boys. You are men," Orlando told his sons. "It is time to take on that responsibility and act accordingly—or do I have to drag you both into a back alley and use my belt on you?"

The truth of it was that their father had never used his belt on either of them in a back alley, or any other area for that matter. But a reply to that declaration was temporarily tabled because Rachel had returned, bringing with her three freshly opened individual bottles of dark beer as well as Matteo's cheeseburger and the new bowl of chips.

Setting down Matteo's meal in front of him and placing the bowl of chips in the center of the table, Rachel proceeded to refill the men's empty beer glasses, beginning with Orlando's.

"Will there be anything else?" she asked with a gregarious smile as she made the rounds between the three men.

Cisco spoke up unexpectedly. "You could settle an argument for us," he said.

Instinct had Matteo shoot his brother a silencing look, but it was already too late.

"What kind of an argument?" Rachel wanted to know, filling Cisco's glass.

"If you had to go out with one of us, which would you choose?" Cisco asked her innocently.

The question seemed to catch her completely off guard, but Rachel managed to recover gracefully without missing a beat.

"That all depends," she responded, going on to Matteo's glass.

"On what?" Cisco asked her before Matteo had a chance to.

Her eyes met Matteo's for one brief and surprisingly intense moment before she looked back at his brother. "On who would ask me first."

"All right," Cisco said quickly, making sure that he got the jump on his brother. "Rachel, would you go out with me tonight?"

It all happened so fast that Matteo felt as if he had just been torpedoed—and sunk—by an enemy sub.

"My shift doesn't end until eight," Rachel replied, still not giving him a definite answer.

It was her way of stalling. It wasn't that she wasn't flattered, because she was—the man who had asked her out just now was every bit as good-looking as his brother—and it wasn't that she was trying to play hard to get, because she wasn't. The reason she was stalling was because she was hoping that the one who had *really* caught her attention, the cute younger brother, who had come to her defense earlier at the other table, would put in his two cents and ask her out, as well. Then she knew who she'd pick.

But from what she could see, the one she had heard referred to as "Matteo" seemed to fold up his tent and just withdraw, allowing his brother to have total access to the entire playing field.

In this case, that meant her, Rachel thought.

"Perfect," Cisco was saying, referring to when her shift ended. "I'll be waiting out front."

Ever since she'd left her home in Austin five years ago, Rachel had been somewhat leery when it came to dating. She'd already gone through her ugly-duckling period and her swan period, during which time she had preened and posed, absorbing each and every flattering word that was sent her way, and viewing it as gospel.

But in time she had learned that those compliments were just empty, meaningless words, easily spoken and even more easily forgotten. She had more important things on her agenda than dating these days. She was busy not just finding herself, but also finding her place in the scheme of things.

Her place in the world.

She was working here as a hostess, but she had recently won an internship at the new Horseback Hollow office of the Fortune Foundation, which had opened its doors several weeks ago. As of yet, the office was still not fully up and running, but she intended to be there right from the start, learning everything she could from the ground up.

Her plan was to make something of herself.

To that end, she was going to continue with both positions, amassing as much money as she could. Her father had offered to support her when she'd left home, as he well could, but she had refused his money. She wanted to make it on her own so that no one else could take the credit—or the blame—for what she had become. It would be all on her, one way or another.

She might not appear so to the patrons seated here

at the Cantina, but she was fiercely dedicated, not to mention full of pride.

Ordinarily, this sort of a work agenda would leave a person with no room for anything else, but she knew that having some sort of a social life was important. She supposed this "date" tonight qualified as just that.

She would have preferred being asked out by the younger hunk, but the one who *did* ask her out wasn't exactly shabby, either. Who knew? Maybe she would wind up having a better time with him than Mr. Cheeseburger, she mused

So Rachel nodded and gave the man who had just asked her out a smile.

"All right, if we're going to go out, I'm going to need to know your name," she told him.

Cisco inclined his head in a polite, surprisingly formal bow as he said, "Francisco Mendoza at your service." Raising his eyes to hers, he added, "Everybody calls me Cisco."

"Then I guess I'll just have to join the crowd," she told him. With that, she looked at the other two occupants of the table. "Since I'm taking names, you are—" she asked Matteo.

"A day late and a dollar short," Cisco supplied before Matteo could answer her.

If looks could kill, the one that Matteo slanted at him would have completely vaporized Cisco in under ten seconds. The scowl abated somewhat as he turned to look at the hostess and told her, "Matteo Mendoza."

"And I am Orlando Mendoza," Orlando told her. In typical old-fashioned, courtly manner, Orlando rose slightly in his chair and bent forward so that he could take her hand in his. He brought her hand to his lips and kissed it as per the custom of his ancestors.

Rather than appear amused, Rachel looked touched and just slightly in awe.

"Mendoza," Rachel repeated, then asked, "Brothers?" as her eyes swept over all three men.

"You are only partially right." Orlando laughed, fully aware that the young woman had asked the question tongue-in-cheek. "And partially a flatterer." He glanced at Cisco and told his son, "This one can hold her own against you."

Cisco's eyes were filled with humor as well as a healthy measure of appreciation as they met hers. "I'm sure she can."

Realizing that she had already spent way too much time at one table, Rachel flashed another quick smile at the trio and began to withdraw, saying, "I'd love to talk some more, but I've got another order up," before she turned on her heel and left.

"And that, little brother," Cisco said as soon as he felt that the hostess was out of earshot, "is how it's done."

Matteo looked at his older sibling, more than a little annoyed at the latter's presumption. "I don't need pointers. And even if I did, it wouldn't be from you."

"Touchy, touchy," Cisco observed with a pitying shake of his head. "You might not be aware of it, little brother, but you definitely are in need of something." He dug into the chicken enchiladas before him. "I just beat you to the punch with Rachel—and the worst part of it is, you let me."

"Beat me to the punch," Matteo repeated incredulously. "Is that what all this is to you? A game? Just a game?"

Cisco refused to get embroiled in an argument, especially one that didn't look as if it could have a clear winner—at least not verbally. He took another bite before saying anything in reply.

"What it is, is invigorating," Cisco told him. "And I intend to have a really good time with the fair Rachel."

Matteo's scowl grew deeper. "If you know what's good for you, you'd better treat her like a lady," he warned Cisco,

"Or what?" Cisco asked, curious as to just where this conversation was going. "You'll beat me up?" Orlando felt that he had sat by in silence long enough. The last thing he wanted was to see this escalate beyond a few hot words traded. Even that was too much.

"Stop it, you two. You are brothers. Remember that," Orlando ordered. "And Cisco, you had better behave like a gentleman with this girl. I will not stand for anything less," he warned his older son.

Cisco didn't want to provoke his father, but the whole thing had made him curious. His father must have sown a few wild oats in his day. There was still a hint of a wicked twinkle left in his eye.

"Don't you remember being young once, Dad?" Cisco asked him.

Orlando made no effort to deny it. "Yes, I do, which is exactly why I am saying this to you now." And then he turned his attention to Matteo. "And you, you have no business telling your brother what to do after you neglected to act according to your own feelings."

Matteo just looked at him, mystified.

"She was waiting for you to say something," he told Matteo. "And you let her slip through your fingers."

Matteo had no idea she was anywhere *near* his fingers to begin with. He had just been working up his courage to engage her in a conversation when Cisco all but pounced on the hostess.

"If you ask me, the better man won," Cisco commented to his father with just a hint of a smirk directed at Matteo.

To be honest—and he was, in the depths of his own heart—he had only asked the hostess out because he saw that Matteo was exhibiting interest in her. Beating him to the punch was, he thought, a good way to light a fire under his brother and get him moving so that the next time, Matteo would be the one who was first to ask her out.

"No one asked you," Matteo snapped.

Orlando looked from one son to the other and wearily shook his head. "You know, perhaps I was too hasty to try to convince you boys to move out here to live. The peace and quiet I had for all those months made me forget how you two were always going at one another when you were growing up. Apparently you haven't outgrown that trait."

Cisco laughed. "I see right through you, Dad. You can talk and complain all you want, but admit it. You missed having us around, competition and all—not that it was ever much of a competition once I decided to throw my hat into the ring." He gave Matteo a smug, superior look that he knew would bother the younger man.

"You're delusional," Matteo told him.

"And you have no memory of things at all. Otherwise, you'd know I was right. If I set my sights on something or someone, the game is already over because, for all intents and purposes, I have won it. All that remains is to collect my winnings," Cisco concluded. He secretly watched Matteo from beneath hooded eyes to see if his words had succeeded in pushing his brother into action. In his opinion, there were times when his little brother was too laid-back. Goading him this way was for his own good. And if not, well, it was Matteo's loss, right?

"Enough," Orlando warned. "I invited you two here to have a nice family meal—so eat!" He looked from one son to the other. After a beat, both complied with his command.

Orlando found the silence gratifying and refreshing. At least now he could hear himself think.

And what he was thinking about was how nice the silence was.

Chapter Three

Rachel closed the door to her apartment behind her and walked into the kitchen. A minute later, she did a U-turn and crossed back to the door. Not to open it again in hopes of catching the man who had just dropped her off because she'd had second thoughts about not asking him in for a drink, but to flip the top lock into place to ensure her safety. The original lock that came with the door was rather flimsy at best.

Five years and security was still an afterthought for her, Rachel thought with a shake of her head.

That was because five years ago, she was living with her seven siblings in a palatial home in Austin. The servants who took care of the house were the ones who made sure doors were locked and everything was always secured. The entire house and grounds were wired with a state-of-the-art security system.

It had been a whole other world then. As one of Gerald Robinson's daughters, her every need had been anticipated and met. Had she wanted merely to float through life, doing nothing more strenuous than enjoying herself and contributing nothing to the world around her, that option had been there for her to take.

But she had always been the stubborn one who wanted to make her own way, earn her own money, *be* her own person. And never more than now—for herself as well as to atone for her father's indiscretions.

Maybe, Rachel mused as she stepped out of her high heels on the way to her tiny bedroom and more comfortable clothes, that earlier way of life had jaded her somewhat, spoiling her for the actual realities of life.

What other reason could there be for her feeling like this after the evening she had just had?

Cisco Mendoza had been as good as his word, waiting for her outside the Cantina when she'd walked out at a few minutes after eight o'clock tonight.

Any other woman would have felt like Cinderella, being whisked off not in a coach that had formerly been a pumpkin but in a shiny, fully loaded black luxury SUV. When she'd asked him where they were going, he'd given her a sexy wink and said in an equally sexy voice that it was a surprise.

She had to admit to herself that *that* had made her a little nervous. Growing up in Austin as the child of a very rich man, her mother and the family housekeeper had made her and her siblings acutely aware of being on their guard against possible kidnappers. Having money did not come without a certain downside.

She was fairly certain that Cisco Mendoza didn't

know about her real background—although she couldn't be 100 percent sure—but then again, there were other reasons for women to go missing.

Cisco must have noticed her tension, because several minutes into their road trip, he laughed and told her where they were going. He was taking her to Vicker's Corners, a town that was roughly twenty miles away and had once been as quaint as Horseback Hollow. But the citizens of Vicker's Corners had chosen to embrace progress, and the town was now well on its way to becoming far more urban than rural.

"I'm taking you to The Garden," he'd added. And then, just in case she wasn't aware what that was—she was, but she pretended she wasn't because he seemed to delight in surprising her—he went on to tell her, "It's a trendy little bistro. I thought you might like to have a little change of pace. It's different from The Hollows Cantina," he promised.

She knew he meant it was more romantic than the upscale restaurant where she worked. Apparently Cisco Mendoza was pulling out all the stops.

She wished her heart was in it—but it wasn't, no matter how hard she tried.

She'd told him that she appreciated his thoughtfulness, then felt the need to point one little fact out, careful to keep it generalized so that he didn't know she was well-informed about the restaurant in question.

"If it's so trendy, wouldn't getting a reservation on the spur of the moment be really difficult? They're probably booked way in advance." She made it sound as if she was guessing, but the truth was that she *knew* for a fact The Garden was booked solid.

Cisco's grin had gotten wider at that point—and, if possible, sexier.

Another wink only intensified that impression, especially when he said, "Leave that part to me. I've got a few strings I can pull. That should be able to get us in."

She was surprised that he was being secretive about that connection of his. She knew better than to pry and try to find out anything beyond what was being volunteered. She was just rather stunned that Cisco wasn't trying to impress her with his mysterious connection.

But that wasn't the real problem as she saw it. The bistro had indeed turned out to be trendy as well as really captivating. It had stained-glass windows, copper ceiling tiles and a vintage art-nouveau crystal chandelier in the entryway.

Moreover, the food was perfect, the conversation was interesting and Cisco was charming, funny and a complete gentleman from start to finish. The date didn't end abruptly or last too long. In the words of Goldilocks, Rachel thought, changing into a pair of jeans and a baggy sweatshirt, it was "just right."

So why had she left Cisco at the door, hotfooting it inside and *not* inviting him in, not making herself available to be kissed good-night?

As she went in, Cisco had acted as if there was nothing out of the ordinary going on, but she could tell that she had surprised him—and disappointed the man, as well.

Rachel walked back out into her living room and flopped down on the sofa. Picking up her remote control, she turned on the TV and automatically began flipping through channels.

She was searching for something—*anything*—to distract her.

Rachel frowned, wondering if there was something wrong with her.

It had been a perfectly nice date, and she had had a perfectly nice time. Granted, there hadn't been a magical spark of chemistry blowing her away, but hey, that was lightning in a bottle, right? Finding something like that was exceptionally rare.

Especially since her mind kept drifting off, envisioning that *other* Mendoza at her side instead of his equally handsome, equally intelligent older brother.

Right up to the end, as she waited on their table earlier today, she kept hoping that Matteo would be the one who would ask her out or, barring that, the one who ultimately showed up in Cisco's place, murmuring vague apologies for his brother and saying something about Cisco being unavoidably detained.

She had found out fairly early in their time together tonight that Cisco was a real-estate investor. So being detained by an important deal was perfectly plausible.

But Cisco hadn't been unavoidably detained, and Matteo hadn't come to take his brother's place. Cisco had been the one waiting for her, the one who followed her home so that she could leave her car there and then ride in his as they went out.

On paper, the man was perfect—and very easy on the eyes, as well. But she heard no bells ringing and no banjos playing when they were alone together. And she really didn't want to settle for anything less than bells and banjos. More than anything else, she wanted a magical relationship—or nothing at all.

It was just as well that it had been Cisco tonight and not Matteo, she told herself, still flipping channels and looking for something numbing and mindless to help her unwind. Cisco had told her that his younger brother was a pilot "like our father." She felt that flying was somewhat risky, and flying for a living just increased that risk.

The last thing she needed was to lose her heart to someone who had a dangerous occupation and might not be there in a week or a month.

This way, there were no unnecessary complications for her to deal with. Just a nice date. End of story, she told herself.

"Face it, Rach. This is *not* the time for you to get involved with anyone." First, she had to get her life in gear and on track—find out where she was going with this Foundation internship she'd taken on. Once that was settled, *then* she could think about getting romantically involved with someone and falling in love, she thought, giving herself a mental pep talk since she had no one to turn to for any sort of support. "Don't go putting the cart before the horse. Remember, you've got a plan and order is everything."

It made for a good argument, she thought, watching channels as they whizzed by.

But deep down in her soul, she wasn't completely convinced.

Just as she had anticipated, Rachel didn't sleep all that well following her date. Every time she managed to doze off, her brain would conjure up fragments of dreams.

For the most part, they had to do with her evening out. But oddly enough, instead of the charismatic and confident Cisco, she saw Matteo at her side.

The dreams seemed so vivid that she felt they were actually happening—until she would wake up and find herself in her bed.

Sweating profusely—and very much alone.

After she'd gone through three such cycles, Rachel gave up all attempts at getting any sort of decent rest.

Besides, she reasoned, it was actually already too late for that. Her alarm was set to go off at seven-thirty. That was in less than another hour. She was going to work at the Fortune Foundation this morning, and she wanted to get there early, before her workday actually started. She wanted to absorb everything she could about the company.

Rachel already knew that the Foundation had been founded in the memory of Fortune patriarch Ryan Fortune, a man who had been a firm believer in paying it forward. He had lived his life that way, personally doing just that at every opportunity.

She'd learned that from the people who had been chosen to run the Horseback Hollow branch of the Fortune Foundation: Christopher Fortune Jones and his new wife, Kinsley.

The couple were returning from their honeymoon today, and Rachel wanted to be right there when they came in—not just to welcome them back, but to be able to listen to everything Christopher had to say.

She sympathized with Christopher and the way he had initially felt about the Fortunes when he had discovered that he and his siblings were actually directly related to the wealthy family. He had learned about this unexpected connection not all that long ago, and it had turned his entire life upside down until he finally made peace with the information.

That had taken a bit of doing on his part, as had adjusting to the fact that his mother, Jeanne Marie, was actually one third of a set of triplets. She and her sister had been given up for adoption. Her brother, James Michael, had grown up not knowing a thing about his two sisters, with only the vaguest memory that they existed.

It was through his relentless efforts to find them that his two sisters were told of their true identities. Both women took it a lot better than their families did at first.

Amazing how being part of that family created such drama for some people, Rachel couldn't help thinking.

The next moment, she pushed the thought aside.

She couldn't just sit around, contemplating life's little tricks and secrets. She had a job waiting for her. A job that *wouldn't* be waiting long if she started coming in late—or calling in sick.

Now, where had that last thought come from? Rachel upbraided herself. It certainly hadn't been on her mind a moment ago.

This was what happened when she broke with her routine, she chided herself. Last night had been an aberration from her normal course of operations, and now she was paying the price by feeling just a little bit better than death warmed over.

Or maybe just as bad.

Knowing she needed a boost, Rachel stopped in the kitchen to pour herself a cup of coffee. Her coffeemaker was ready for her, as she'd set the timer to brew at the ungodly hour of four-thirty in the morning.

Closing her eyes as she took her first sips, Rachel gave herself a moment to allow the jet-black hot liquid to go slowly coursing through her veins, bringing everything in its path to attention.

How did people live before coffee was invented? she idly wondered.

"Better," she pronounced after a few more moments had gone by. She felt almost human now.

Fortified, Rachel set the cup down on the counter and hurried off to take a quick shower.

It was only belatedly, several moments later, that she realized a face had flashed through her mind's eye when she'd closed her eyes to savor her coffee.

The face belonged to Matteo Mendoza.

This time she didn't bother trying to deny it or to talk herself out of her obvious attraction to the man. Instead, she just found herself wondering if she was going to see Matteo again.

And if so, when.

Rachel made it to the Fortune Foundation office at ten to nine, approximately fifteen minutes before the newlyweds arrived.

Their attempt to slip in quietly was quickly thwarted. Several of the other people who worked in the office saw them the moment they walked in and greeted them with hearty words of welcome.

Rachel added her voice to theirs, genuinely delighted to see the happy couple.

"Welcome back, you two," Rachel cried, speaking up to be heard above the rest. "We missed you."

Christopher laughed as he looked in her direction and replied, "No offense, but we didn't miss you."

Chris looked back at his wife, and Rachel knew exactly what he'd meant with his last remark. That Kinsley filled up his whole world and there was no space left over for anyone else, so no one else could possibly be missed.

Rachel felt envy pricking her. The love Christopher and Kinsley had for one another was almost visible.

She caught herself wondering if she was *ever* going to find someone who loved her like that—someone whom *she* could love like that, she silently added.

If the way she'd felt yesterday evening after her date was any indication, the answer to that was a depressing but resounding no.

Pushing that daunting thought aside—and knowing that the couple undoubtedly was on cloud nine and not quite ready to descend and start working just yet—Rachel came over to them.

"So, how did the big family reunion go?" Rachel asked him. When Christopher looked at her, clearly puzzled, she clarified her question. "At the wedding. That was the first time you actually met some of the other members of the Fortune family—your family," she corrected herself. "Right?"

Christopher nodded, the look on his face telling her that he was partially reliving the scene in his mind. "Right."

"And?" Rachel prompted him eagerly.

"And," Christopher continued after taking in a deep breath, "it was kind of rocky at first. I wasn't sure how they'd all react to all of us, or to me," he said glibly. He spared no words criticizing his own behavior. "I mean, I hadn't exactly welcomed the news with open arms initially myself. To tell you the truth, I was pretty surprised that they even showed up at the wedding."

"But your mother invited them," Rachel pointed out.

"That made no difference." And then he smiled. The smile was equal parts humor and relief. "But just as when I first met most of them in Red Rock last year, they turned out to be a lot more understanding than I expected. I can truthfully say that they are a *very* nice bunch of people as a group *and* individually," he added. "To be honest, if I had to pick my own family, I couldn't have done a better job than picking the Fortunes. They're charitable and decent, and they don't behave as if they feel they're privileged or something particularly special."

Christopher abruptly stopped talking. "You've got a strange look on your face, Rachel. Is there something on your mind you'd like to talk about?"

Yes, there is. But you didn't come back to work to be burdened by my problems.

"No," she said out loud. "I was just curious."

But maybe now wasn't the time to satisfy her curiosity. After all, there was the matter of that little gold band on his left hand. That undoubtedly would take him a bit of time to get used to, too—even *after* the honeymoon.

For now, Rachel decided, she was just going to keep a low profile and do her job—or jobs, she corrected herself, since, just for a moment, she had forgotten about her job at the Cantina.

The second she thought of the Cantina, an image of Matteo flashed through her mind. Something else she couldn't think about right now, she silently chided.

With effort, she focused on what she had to do right this moment, at the Foundation—but it wasn't easy. Thoughts of Matteo continued to tease her brain.

Chapter Four

It took a few more minutes before things settled back down and the office returned to its former rhythm, with everyone focusing on preparing for next month.

Rachel hardly had a chance to sit at her desk again when there was a slight commotion at the outer door. Since the Foundation wasn't scheduled to open until April 1, they were still closed to the general public.

As far as she knew, everyone who was supposed to be here *was* here.

So who were these two people, a man and a woman, walking into the second-floor office?

Looking at them more closely, Rachel was struck that although the woman was a blue-eyed blonde and the man had dark hair and dark eyes, both bore a striking resemblance to Christopher. Were they part of his family? she wondered.

The way he greeted the duo the next minute answered her question for her.

"Hey, look what the cat dragged in." Christopher laughed, crossing the room to them with his wife.

"I told you we were ready to come do whatever it is that you're doing here," the man reminded him, looking around the room as if to get properly oriented.

Christopher had an inch on the other man, and his dirty-blond hair was more like the woman's. He looked genuinely pleased to see both of them.

"You're not fooling me," Christopher told the man. "You just think you can hide out here, away from our crazy matchmaking relatives. I can tell you now, it won't do either one of you any good. They'll find you."

Having said that, Christopher glanced around at the other people in the office, all of whom were looking at the two latest arrivals, clearly wondering who they were. Their curiosity was short-lived, thanks to Christopher.

"Hey, everybody, I'd like you all to meet my big brother, Galen, and my little sister, Delaney. Study them carefully. They're the last of their kind," he declared with no small amount of amusement.

Delaney frowned. "You make us sound like we're about to go extinct."

"Well, aren't you?" Christopher asked with a straight face. "Hey, don't blame me," he pretended to protest. "You two started it by calling yourself 'the last remaining singles.'"

"Well, what would you call us?" Delaney wanted to know. "Now that you and our other three siblings have gone to the other side and joined the ranks of the happily married, everybody thinks Galen and I should follow suit and hurry up and get married—like, yesterday." She tossed her head, sending her blond hair flying over her shoulder in one swift, graceful movement.

"Neither one of us is in any hurry to tie the knot—certainly not just to please the rest of the family," she informed Christopher—*not* for the first time. "I, for one, intend to enjoy my freedom for as long as I possibly can. I *like* being my own boss and coming and going as I please."

He'd been of a like mind once, Christopher thought. But that was before he'd fallen in love with the most beautiful woman in the world.

"You make marriage sound like a prison sentence," Christopher told her.

Delaney looked across the room and saw her new sister-in-law talking to one of the workers. "No offense to your lovely wife, but…" Delaney deliberately allowed her voice to trail off.

"How about you?" she asked, moving closer to Rachel. "Don't you agree that it's really great to be single?"

There were times, especially when she saw how happy some couples were, that Rachel longed to be in a committed relationship. Before they had locked horns, vying for the same position—the one that she now currently held—she and Shannon Singleton had been friends. Shannon had been the very first friend she'd made in Horseback Hollow. Now her friend was engaged to one of the British Fortune relations, Oliver Fortune Hayes.

Another thing she couldn't help thinking was that

she missed having a friend, missed the intimate camaraderie of having someone to share secrets with, or just to talk to for hours on end about nothing in particular.

Oh, she was friendly when their paths crossed, but that was rare these days. Shannon was much too busy with her new relationship and her new life. For the most part, it didn't bother her too much. But there were times, when she was home, that she would have given *anything* to have a real friend to talk to.

Someone like Christopher's baby sister, she thought suddenly.

There was something about the young woman that made Rachel take an instant liking to her the moment Delaney had opened her mouth.

There weren't many people she felt an immediate and strong connection to, Rachel realized, but Delaney was someone who could definitely qualify if she was interested in reciprocating the feeling.

"Being single has its moments," Rachel finally said in response to Delaney's question.

"Not exactly a ringing endorsement," Delaney allowed philosophically, "but I'll take it." The younger woman gave her a wide, infectious grin. "You obviously know my name—Chris's voice is kind of hard to block out—but I don't know yours," she told Rachel as she raised one expressive eyebrow, waiting.

"Rachel," Rachel answered. Belatedly, she put out her hand. "Rachel Robinson."

"Well, Rachel Robinson, I'm very pleased to meet you," Delaney said, warmly shaking her hand. "Maybe you can give me a clearer idea of what it is that we do here, other than look noble while we're doing it," she added with a somewhat bemused smile.

"What we're doing is getting ready. We're not open yet," Christopher informed his sister, cutting in before Rachel had a chance to make any sort of a reply. "Our official opening is set for next month. April," he added for complete clarity. "So right now, we're just running around, scrambling to get all systems up and running."

Delaney nodded, as if something had just clicked into place in her head. "Is that why you said you didn't care how casual I dressed and that jeans and boots would even be a good idea?"

"Did it take you that long to figure out?" Galen asked with a laugh. "I knew Chris was after cheap labor right from the get-go."

"What do you mean, 'cheap'?" Christopher asked. "The word is *free*. At least for now," he added before either one of his siblings could comment or pretend to protest. Turning toward Galen, Christopher deadpanned, "You still have that strong back?"

Rather than instantly answer in the affirmative, Galen's response was a guarded one. "That all depends on what you want done."

Fair enough, Christopher thought. "I've got some desks that are going to need moving."

Galen shook his head. "Then the answer is no. I threw my back out herding cattle," he told his brother.

Christopher's eyes narrowed as he studied Galen's face. He could always tell if his brother was bluffing. "You did not."

For a moment, the expression on Galen's face made the immediate future unclear. And then the oldest of the Fortune Jones clan shrugged, surrendering. "It was worth a shot."

Before they discovered that they were all directly related to the Fortune family thanks to their mother, they had been the Jones family, ranchers who made a living but could never boast that they thought of themselves as being even remotely well-off. Their lives consisted of hard work. Unexpectedly finding out that they were Fortunes with the kind of inheritance that befit someone from that family changed nothing, other than the fact that they now knew they would never be in a hand-to-mouth situation again.

The discovery certainly didn't alter their work ethic, didn't suddenly change them into a family of squanderers. But now, instead of working to keep body and soul together, they worked because ranching was what they enjoyed.

Galen pretended to sigh and acted put-upon. "So when do you want me to get started breaking my back?"

Christopher was about to answer when there was another commotion at the office door. His attention was instantly focused there.

"Could be the furniture arriving now," he told Galen cheerfully.

He was just yanking his older brother's chain. Christopher had no intentions of relying exclusively on his brother to shift around and arrange the furniture. It would be arriving with a crew of moving men in attendance. He just enjoyed giving Galen a hard time while he still could.

But when the doors into the office opened, it wasn't to admit a team of movers bringing the rest of the furniture for this office—or any of the other Foundation offices in the newly constructed two-story building.

Instead of moving men, Orlando and Matteo Mendoza came walking in.

Rachel felt her heart reacting the second she looked up and saw Matteo. It took her almost a full minute for her to regain her composure.

What was he doing here?

By the look on Delaney's face, she'd noted the sudden change in Rachel. But mercifully, she made no comment, which only further cemented the budding friendship in Rachel's mind. To her, friends knew things about friends without asking outright.

Almost automatically, Rachel rose to her feet and found herself slowly moving closer to the front door and the two men who had entered.

If she was surprised to see Matteo, he looked twice as surprised to see her.

Perhaps, Rachel thought, he looked a little *too* surprised.

Had he somehow known she'd be here today?

She tried to remember if she had said anything to Cisco last night about having to work here at the Foundation's office today.

But even if she had, the little voice in her head that came equipped with a large dose of common sense maintained, why would Cisco have shared that information with his younger brother? From the interaction she had witnessed yesterday, the two had an ongoing rivalry, competing with one another over just about *everything*.

But if that was the case, then what was Matteo doing here?

It didn't make any sense to her.

"What can I do for you?" Christopher was asking the two men as he crossed the office to get to them.

"It's what we're here to do for you," Orlando corrected him. The older man nodded his head toward Matteo. "My stubborn mule of a son and I are here to deliver a shipment of supplies for your office from your Red Rock headquarters."

Not willing to be mischaracterized, Matteo chimed in, "My more stubborn father suffered a bad injury last year and really should still be taking it easy instead of making these cargo flights," Matteo explained. "I came along in order to ensure that he wasn't taking on too much too soon. I'm also a pilot," he added, wanting Rachel to know that he wasn't just ineptly tagging along after his father but had a true purpose as well as a true vocation.

Orlando snorted like a parent who was trying patiently to endure the know-it-all attitude of his well-meaning children. "This one thinks I'll have a heart attack and he'll have to grab the controls and heroically land the plane." Orlando puffed up his chest ever so slightly and added, "Apparently he doesn't realize his father is as strong as an ox."

"Yeah and just as stubborn as one," Matteo interjected. He turned toward Christopher. "If you just tell me where you keep your dolly, I'll load it up and bring the supplies up for you."

"I'd appreciate that," he said to Matteo. Turning toward Rachel, he recruited her help. "Rachel, would you show Orlando where we keep the dolly? Then bring him back to the storeroom when he's ready so he can stack the supplies there." He glanced at Orlando.

He had forgotten just how much he had ordered. "Is it a large shipment?"

Orlando nodded. "I would say so, yes."

The smile on Christopher's lips was spontaneous as well as wide.

"It's all coming together," he announced, partly to the people in the office, partly to himself.

While ranching had initially been a way of life for him, running a branch of his newly discovered family's charitable foundation seemed like a very noble endeavor to him. And the more involved he became, the more committed to the cause he felt.

"We keep the dolly in the storeroom," Rachel told Matteo. "Come on, follow me. I'll show you where it is."

Matteo fell into step with her as she walked quickly to the end of the floor and the storeroom.

"So, you work here, too?" he asked her, sounding somewhat puzzled.

That Matteo asked the question disappointed her a little. It meant that this meeting really was just an accident rather than something he had deliberately orchestrated.

What was she thinking, assuming that Matteo had gone through complex machinations just to get a glimpse of her again? Sometimes a chance meeting was a chance meeting and nothing more, she told herself.

But the fact that it was obviously true in this case stung her a little. The scenario she had put together in her head had been far more romantic.

Grow up, she chided herself.

Looking at Matteo, she realized that he was waiting for some sort of an answer.

"I just started working here," she replied. "The Foundation doesn't officially open to the public until next month."

Matteo was still trying to piece things together. He knew so little about the woman who had captivated him with no effort whatsoever. He had deliberately been avoiding Cisco this morning because he didn't want to take a chance on hearing his brother brag about what had gone on last night.

"So, yesterday was your last day at the Cantina?" he asked.

That was a shame, he thought. He'd given serious consideration to dropping in there tomorrow, supposedly for lunch but actually just to see her again. Now it looked as if that plan wasn't destined to make it off the ground.

Opening the door to the storeroom, Rachel gestured toward the dolly—located right in front—and stepped out of Matteo's way.

"No, actually, it wasn't. My job at the Cantina is really part-time, and I'm keeping both jobs, at least for a while," she told him. Just saying it made her feel tired. But this wasn't about getting her beauty rest. It was about her future and getting ahead. "I want to see where this is going before I make any major decisions about my life."

Pushing the dolly out of the room, he followed Rachel toward the elevator. "Have you always been this ambitious?" he asked her.

She had to admit that this was an entirely new direction for her. When she'd moved out here, she hadn't a clue on how to start rebuilding herself—or even how to earn a living. All she knew was that she wasn't running toward something—at least, not at first—but *from* something.

"No, I wasn't," she told him, pressing the down arrow beside the elevator. "You should have seen me five years ago." She recalled all the empty partying, the meaningless kisses and even more meaningless words that had been exchanged. "I was a slug," she confessed with a self-deprecating laugh.

Matteo didn't believe it for a moment. He considered himself a fair to middling judge of character, and Rachel Robinson was a woman with a purpose. He would lay odds that she always had been.

"I sincerely doubt that," he told her, dismissing her words. "But I would have liked to have seen you five years ago," he admitted.

Rachel couldn't think of a reason why he would have wanted to do that. "To compare then and now?" she guessed.

"No. If I *had* seen you five years ago, that means I would have known you for five years." And he would have been able to get her attention before Cisco had a chance to move in on her. "But I guess since you live here and I grew up in Miami, that wouldn't have exactly been possible," he concluded.

"No," she agreed, "it wouldn't have." But that didn't mean that she wouldn't have wanted it to be possible, she added silently.

As Matteo stepped into the elevator, pushing the dolly before him, he was surprised to see Rachel get on with him. He'd just assumed that she would wait for him to return to the storeroom with the supplies. "You're coming with me?"

"If you don't mind."

His smile was very wide as he told her, "No, I don't mind. I don't mind at all."

Chapter Five

"What happened?" Rachel asked Matteo as they stepped out of the elevator with the dolly on the ground floor.

Since the question seemed to come out of the blue, Matteo looked at her, puzzled. He wasn't sure what Rachel was asking him. In all honesty, he might have been so captivated by her proximity that he'd completely zoned out for a moment, thereby missing a possibly vital part of the conversation.

He would have attempted to bluff his way out of it, but that could have been successful only if he'd had an iota of a clue what she was referring to. And he really didn't.

When in doubt, his father had taught all of them, honesty was the best policy.

"I'm afraid I don't know what you mean," he told

Rachel, feeling more than a little awkward about the admission and hoping that she didn't think he was a complete idiot.

She flashed a smile that corkscrewed its way directly into his gut, tightening it.

"I'm sorry," she said. "I have a tendency to start questions in my head, leaving vital parts out when I engage my mouth. You told my boss that you came along with your father because you were afraid he hadn't sufficiently recovered from his injury. I was just curious about what kind of an injury it was."

Before I engage my mouth. The words she'd used echoed in his brain as he looked at that very same mouth now. He would have liked to engage that mouth in his own way, he couldn't help thinking.

With effort, he made himself focus on the question she had asked and not on the woman herself.

"It's a long story," he told her as they got off the elevator and headed past the reception area, toward the front doors. "The short version is that his plane malfunctioned and he crashed. The doctors thought his recovery was amazing. I just didn't want him to overdo things. He doesn't like owning up to a weakness, especially a physical one. But he *is* human, so things can happen that are beyond his control."

They approached a silver midsize van parked several feet from the building's entrance.

"I'm stunned that your father actually got into a plane and flew again after that," Rachel said.

Matteo smiled to himself. She caught herself thinking that he had a really gorgeous smile. It was the kind that lit up the immediate area around him—and her.

"My father is probably the most bullheaded man

who ever walked the earth," Matteo told her. "He does *not* like backing away from any sort of a challenge— and he's been a pilot for most of his life. Flying is second nature to him, like breathing."

Rachel nodded intently, as if absorbing every word. "I see. Well, good for him," she declared with feeling. "Sometimes being stubborn like that is all we have to see us through."

Matteo wondered if she was talking about herself rather than his father. Something in her voice made him think she at least related to the experience.

Rachel paused on the sidewalk while he unlocked the back of his father's van.

Climbing inside, he moved the supplies his father had flown in, dragging them closer to the bumper. Then he jumped down again. Box by box, he loaded a third of the supplies onto the dolly. A third was all that it would hold at one time.

"Okay, let's go," he told her.

Rachel looked at the back of the van as he pushed the doors closed. "What about the rest of it?" she wanted to know.

Positioning himself behind it, he began to push the loaded dolly toward the front entrance. "I'm going to have to come back. There's no way I can get the supplies into the storeroom all in one trip."

"Oh," she murmured. Rachel saw it as an opportunity to spend a little more time with Matteo than she'd initially anticipated. Not that he actually needed her help, but since Christopher hadn't specifically told her to show Matteo the storeroom and then come right back, she gave herself a little leeway in the matter. After all, Matteo might have a question for her regarding the supplies.

Orlando, still talking with Christopher, glanced in their direction as they got off the elevator and made their way toward the storeroom.

"If you have an extra dolly," Orlando said, speaking up and addressing the words to Christopher, "we can get the supplies up here twice as fast."

But Christopher shook his head. "Sorry, we've got only the one. But there's no reason to hurry," he assured Orlando. "I figure once we're open, things are really going to start hopping. Until then, we can take life at a bit of a slower pace."

Orlando nodded, as if in agreement, but he didn't fool his son. Matteo knew his father was just going along with what Christopher Fortune Jones had said to come across as agreeable. In reality, his father didn't know how to take life at a slower pace.

That wasn't his father's style. The man had worked from the time he had been a nine-year-old boy, growing up on the streets of Juarez in Mexico, looking for a way to help support his family. When his parents had moved the family to Miami the year he turned ten, things hadn't changed for Orlando. The locale might have been different, but his work ethic had stayed the same: work as hard and as much as you could today because tomorrow was an uncertainty.

As they approached the storeroom, Rachel moved slightly ahead of Matteo in order to open the door for him. She quickly ducked inside to give him room to come in with the dolly.

Following her into the storeroom, Matteo righted the dolly and parked it in order move the supplies off and place them on the shelves, which were only half-stocked at this point.

He had a feeling that this trip to the Foundation might just be the first of many. Suddenly the future was beginning to show promise. Thoughts of returning to Miami took a backseat for the time being.

When he finished taking the first load off the dolly, stacking each container on top of others with the same dimensions, he started to leave. Rachel, he noted, was right behind him.

Was she coming with him? Had he said something to make her feel obligated to do that? Matteo felt bad, as if he was putting her out. Guilt began to nibble away at him like a determined chipmunk.

"You know," he told her, "you don't have to come back to the van with me."

"Sure I do," she contradicted him innocently. Then, with a smile that seemed to seal itself immediately to the inside of his heart, she added, "If I stay behind, who's going to press the elevator button for you?"

He laughed at the absurdity of the question, a little of the tension leaving his shoulders. They no longer felt as if they resembled a landing pad.

It almost felt intimate, sharing the moment—and a joke—with her.

"You're right," Matteo responded. "What was I thinking?"

Had she asked *him* that, he would have had to have answered, *I was thinking about you.*

By the time they made the third and final round trip to the sidewalk and back, the van had been completely emptied and this particular storeroom—Matteo learned there were others—filled to capacity.

So much so that there was precious little room in which to maneuver.

Rachel found that out the hard way.

Moving back to get out of Matteo's way, she found that her back was blocked by a huge floor-to-ceiling stack of boxed printer paper. A wall of ink cartridges were right next to the boxes of paper.

Matteo, unaware that she had nowhere to go, attempted to move past her and wound up brushing up against her.

The moment of contact did *not* go unnoticed.

By either of them.

He was acutely aware of brushing against the sweetly supple, heart-melting brunette as every part of him—not just the parts that had made actual contact, but *all* of him—felt as if it was experiencing an electrical surge that seemed to fill every single space in his body.

Had he looked down instead of directly into her beautiful blue eyes, Matteo was certain that he would have seen sparks flying between their bodies.

As it was, she took his very breath away so completely he felt he was in danger of asphyxiating right then and there.

Breathe, idiot, breathe! Matteo silently ordered himself.

He felt his head spinning around for a moment. This tall, willowy young woman had that sort of an effect on him.

Kiss me, Matteo, Rachel silently begged as her body came alive, tingling intensely from the fleeting and all-too-real contact between their two bodies. *Please kiss me.*

Rachel held her breath, hoping.

Praying.

Refusing to budge a fraction of an inch, hoping that would encourage Matteo to make a move.

Her eyes held his. If mental telepathy was an actual thing rather than a myth, Rachel couldn't help thinking, Matteo Mendoza would have already swept her into his arms, held on to her tightly and kissed her soundly. If nothing else, the way she was looking at him would have hypnotized him into making that first move. She could definitely take it from there.

What was *wrong* with him? Matteo silently upbraided himself.

If he were more like Cisco, this would already have been a done deal. He would have pulled this woman whose mere glance set him on fire into his arms like some soap-opera hero, said a few well-articulated words that would have swept her off her feet and then kissed her the way she had never been kissed before.

Matteo continued to berate himself. If he were more like Cisco, he wouldn't be thinking about it. He would be *acting* on it. It would have already been done.

Or perhaps even be ongoing.

So what was to stop him from doing just that? From acting instead of just thinking? Matteo silently demanded of himself.

Come on, Matteo, do it. Go with your instincts and kiss her already.

Making up his mind, Matteo squared his shoulders and then he began to lean into her.

The very air stood still around her.

It's going to happen. He's going to kiss me. Finally! The thought telegraphed itself through her brain as the rest of her grew excited in anticipation.

Every nerve in her body felt like applauding and cheering wildly. She was afraid to move or even breathe.

His mouth was almost on hers, his breath tantalizing her as she felt it on her face.

Do it, Matteo. Do it, Rachel prayed.

Contact seemed totally inevitable.

And then it wasn't.

"So there you are. I was beginning to think you and that dolly had disappeared."

Orlando's voice seemed to almost boom as it rang out through the storeroom. The elder Mendoza was right there, standing in the entrance, larger-than-life and twice as loud.

"How long does it take you to unload a simple shipment?" Orlando wanted to know before he suddenly stopped dead in his tracks, taking in the scenario and what he belatedly realized were the intense vibrations throbbing all around him.

So near and yet so far, Rachel thought, deeply disappointed and struggling not to show it to either of the men within the crammed room.

Matteo's spirits came crashing down, almost oppressing him. "Just finishing up with the last of it, Dad," he responded, doing his best not to snap at his father.

Damn it, Dad, talk about having awful timing, Matteo thought. He caught himself at the last minute, keeping the words from escaping his mouth.

His insides felt as if they were all revved up and humming with absolutely no release in sight.

Matteo thought of following Rachel back to her cubicle to explore further the intense magnetism he felt palpitating between them. If it was any stronger, he was convinced it would have been a visible, solid entity.

His sense of disappointment in the way things had turned out was beyond measure.

She had to admit that she was very surprised a plume of smoke wasn't trailing in her wake. The way Matteo looked at her—never mind that their bodies had brushed against one another—he'd certainly made her feel as if she was not just hot, but that an out-of-control five-alarm fire was raging within her.

And that Matteo was the additional fuel.

Glancing in the glass door as she approached her office, she saw Matteo's reflection. He was following her. And judging by his expression, he was rather determined to have his way.

Oh, please, let it be what I think it might be.

She sent up a silent prayer to the saint of hopeless cases, St. Jude, bartering then and there and promising to send a sizable donation to a charity that bore his name if only her dream scenario became a reality.

It didn't even have to be a long kiss, she bargained. It was possible to contain and lock passion into a small container. Doing so didn't diminish its strength by any means.

She was debating just thrusting herself in Matteo's path so that he had no choice but to grab her to move her out of the way. She wanted to give him an excuse to make contact again. If they remained alone, who knew where this might go?

But before anything promising could happen, her cell phone rang.

The sound, usually a pleasant one to her, was simply jarring this time around, causing her more than a degree of discomfort.

Her intuition told her that the ringing wasn't about to go away. Rachel had a feeling that whoever was on the other end of the call would just keep calling until they got her on the phone, rather than leaving a message on her voice mail. Served her right for turning her phone on. She should have left it off.

"Hello, this is Rachel." The words came to her tongue automatically. She didn't even stop to think about them before speaking.

And then she stiffened as she recognized the voice on the other end. Of all the phone calls for her to get while standing less than three feet away from the object of her budding affection, this was the last one she would have expected—or wanted.

"So your cell phone does work," the male voice said, amused. "You are a very hard lady to reach." The chuckle was deep and throaty, fading into the atmosphere before the man continued. "This is Cisco Mendoza."

"Yes, I realize that," Rachel acknowledged, her voice still sounding a bit stiff.

Matteo caught her intonation and instantly looked at her in utter amazement. A gut feeling told him that she was taking a call from Cisco. The same gut feeling that had urged him to kiss her. That he'd failed to follow the first instinct would be something he feared he was going to regret for the rest of his life. At least.

Speaking again, Cisco's voice carried, despite the fact that she had the cell closer to her and it wasn't on Speaker.

"I had a really great time with you last night," Cisco was saying to her. "I was wondering if you'd like to do it again."

"Do it again?" she echoed. Out of the corner of her eye, she could see Matteo suddenly look her way. Her last words had obviously caught his attention.

Listening.

"Yes. I was hoping that you would be able to go out with me again tonight," Cisco told her. "See if we can recapture that feeling we had last night."

"Um, I'm not sure that I can make it," Rachel said, uncharacteristically stumbling over her own tongue.

She was *not* usually this socially awkward. After all, Cisco was a perfectly nice person who had been a complete gentleman last night. But he didn't make her toes curl or her blood rush. She didn't want to encourage Cisco since there had been no sparks, especially not the kind that she had just felt with Matteo.

But she didn't like being cruel, either. There had to be a painless way to ease out of this situation without hurting the man's ego.

Watching Rachel, Matteo saw the distressed, uncomfortable look on her face. Filling in the blanks and going on what little information he had picked up about her, he realized that Rachel was trying to find a way out of starting a relationship with Cisco without bruising his brother's feelings.

Another reason to really like the woman, he thought.

His brother, Matteo knew, had a skin as thick as a rhino. He doubted there was anything anyone could say to Cisco that would even mildly upset him.

And if, perchance, he was wrong, and getting turned down by Rachel would crush his brother's cavalier spirit, well, those were just the hazards of love and war. These things happened.

He surprised her by putting his hand over hers on the cell. When she looked at him quizzically, he mouthed, *May I?*

Unable to think of a reason why she wouldn't want him to talk to his brother, she nodded and released the cell phone to him. Matteo smiled at her before addressing the person he assumed was on the other end.

"Cisco?"

There was a bewildered pause before Cisco finally responded. He sounded a bit confused when he did. "Is that you, Matteo?"

"Yes, it's me. Rachel can't see you tonight because she's already going out with someone."

"Who?" Cisco challenged him, surprised.

"Me," Matteo told him.

Rachel's mouth dropped open. Had there been a feather available in the immediate area at that very moment, it could have knocked her over.

Easily.

Chapter Six

The silence on the other end of the line stretched out to almost half a minute. Matteo was beginning to think that Cisco had either hung up on him or lost the connection.

He was about to hand the cell back to Rachel when he heard his brother say, "I'm impressed, little brother. You've gotten quicker."

Pulling the phone closer again, Matteo responded, "Yeah, well, sometimes you just have to be."

Out of the corner of his eye, he saw the way Rachel was looking at him. She seemed to be completely stunned. He supposed that announcing to his brother that she was going out with him might have rattled her a little.

Had he scared her off by his assertive behavior? God, he hoped not. This was what he got for acting impulsively, like Cisco.

"You want to talk to Rachel again?" he asked his brother.

"Sure, why not?" Cisco said gamely. As far as Matteo could tell, Cisco sounded amused. What he couldn't fathom was why.

Matteo held out the cell phone to her. "Here," he murmured. "He wants to talk to you again."

Rachel took her phone back, not really knowing what to make of the entire exchange she'd just heard. She definitely wanted to go out with Matteo instead of Cisco, but she didn't like the idea that she—and any input that she might have had on the subject—had been completely usurped in this whole process. Matteo hadn't even asked her to go out. He just seemed to have assumed that she would agree.

That wasn't like him.

Not like him? What are you, lifelong friends? You just met him. How much do you really know about the man? a small voice in her head asked.

The answer to that was a painful "not much." She was going strictly on gut instincts alone. There were times, she knew, when that wasn't nearly enough. This could be one of those times.

"Hello," Rachel said uncertainly as she brought the cell phone closer to her ear.

"Just wanted to wish you luck with my little brother tonight," Cisco told her cheerfully. "Maybe we can go out some other time." He sounded rather confident that they would.

She, however, was of a different opinion. "Maybe," she replied without any indication of how she really felt about that.

"I'll hold you to that." He laughed, then said, "'Bye," and ended the call.

Belatedly, Rachel followed suit.

The second she tucked her phone away in her pocket, Matteo started talking. He sounded somewhat uncomfortable. "Listen, I'm sorry about that." He nodded toward the pocket that contained her cell phone.

"Sorry?" Rachel echoed. She hadn't the slightest idea what Matteo was actually referring to or apologizing for. Was he sorry about taking the phone from her, or was he apologizing for jumping the gun and saying they were going out?

"I know how pushy Cisco can be, and I just wanted to help you out if, for some reason, you didn't want to go out with him." He had to admit that the sound of his brother's voice had been like waving the proverbial red flag in front of a bull. It just set him off, and he had acted rashly. "You don't have to go out with me, either, if you don't want to."

Now she *really* felt confused. Exactly what was he saying?

"So, you're *not* asking me out?" She wanted to pin this Mendoza down. "That wasn't just an oversight on your part? That little step you forgot to take?"

It was his turn to be confused. "What step?" Matteo asked.

"The step where you actually *ask* me out," she responded.

Damn, but she had him all tied up in knots. Just looking at her was scrambling his brain, Matteo thought. He couldn't think straight. He knew he should just let this go and back away, but his need to know got the best of him.

"If I did ask you out," he said slowly, watching her carefully, "what would you say?"

"I don't know," Rachel answered. Granted, it was a lie, because she knew *exactly* what her answer would have been, but she felt he deserved to twist a little in the wind over this. "I never know how I'll react to something until it happens. I guess you'll actually have to ask me out to find out my answer," she informed Matteo glibly.

Talk about putting himself out there, he thought. "You're kidding."

A Mona Lisa smile gently curved her mouth. She was *not* about to back down. "No, I'm not."

"Okay." Taking a moment, Matteo centered himself, focusing on his words and the woman he was saying them to. He asked, "Rachel Robinson, would you do me the honor of allowing me to have the pleasure of your company this evening?"

He sounded so formal. The only thing that was missing was the clank of armor as he took her hand in his just before he asked her out.

Tickled, Rachel smiled broadly at him. These Mendoza men were a complicated lot, she couldn't help thinking. And then she quickly set his mind at ease. "I thought you'd never ask!"

"Just so I'm sure, is that a yes?"

"Well, it's not a no," she deadpanned, then laughed as she confirmed, "Yes, that's a yes."

Matteo's face lit up. "Great," he said enthusiastically. "What time do you get off from here?"

"Five," she answered. She knew that once the

Foundation was open, her hours might be more structured. But for now, it was a nine-to-five job.

Matteo nodded, as if that was what he'd expected to hear. "Why don't you give me your address and I'll pick you up at six? Unless that's not enough time to get ready," he quickly interjected.

Now, that was certainly thoughtful, she thought, impressed. "That's enough time even if I was going to rebuild myself from top to bottom," she assured him. Rattling off her address to him, she then asked, "What should I wear?"

"Clothes would be good, but it's up to you." Okay, maybe he was channeling *too* much of his brother now, Matteo lectured himself silently.

He noticed with relief that Rachel appeared to be amused more than anything else.

"I've got that part down already. What *kind* of clothes?" she wanted to know. His brother had taken her to a fancy, romantic restaurant in Vicker's Corners, but she had a feeling that unless Matteo was planning to compete with his brother on every level, he wasn't the structured, romantic-restaurant type.

"Casual," Matteo replied. Then, in case that wasn't enough information, he specified, "Boots-and-jeans casual."

Since those were the clothes she tended to favor, Rachel was more than happy to go along with his suggestion.

"Boots and jeans it is."

It was amazing how many different tops a person could try on and discard within the space of fifty-three minutes, Rachel thought, looking at the disarrayed piles on her bed. She'd had no problem with the bottom half of her outfit. Picking out which jeans she was wearing was a snap—the boot-cut ones that hugged her curves.

And she didn't own a large selection of boots— there were only two pairs on the floor of her closet.

But tops, well, that was another story. She had a couple dozen of those—if not more—and every one had something wrong with it.

Or so it seemed when she pulled each one out of her closet and critically looked it over.

Running out of time, Rachel knew she finally had to make her choice, picking the last top she'd pulled on, mainly by default. It was either that one or nothing—and Matteo was at her door right now, ringing the doorbell.

Her heart seemed to be doing a little Irish jig in her chest. Nonetheless, she gave herself a quick once-over in the mirror, murmured, "Here goes nothing," and hurried to open the door.

Matteo had been preparing his opening lines all the way from his father's house to her apartment. He changed a word here, substituted a word there.

When Rachel opened her door to admit him, he promptly forgot every single one of those words. Looking at her had knocked every one of them out of his head like so many dried grains of rice raining down on a harsh terrain. All he could say was "Wow."

As it turned out, he couldn't have come up with a better word to use. Hearing the single word, rendered as an assessment, brought a huge smile to her lips.

He liked the way her eyes lit up when she smiled.

"Thank you. That's the nicest thing anyone has ever said to me."

Matteo caught himself thinking of his brother. Cisco seemed to possess a silver tongue, charming his way into—as well as out of—many a situation. He was fairly certain Cisco had laid it on thick last night.

"I doubt that," he responded, taking a single step just inside her apartment.

"Where are we going?" she wanted to know, grabbing her jacket and her purse before heading back to him and out the door.

"How do you feel about horseback riding?" Matteo asked her, paying close attention to the expression on her face more than the words that would be coming out of her mouth. He didn't want her just going along with something because he suggested it. He wanted her to be enthusiastic about the evening.

Taking out her key, Rachel locked her door. His question brought visions of home instantly to her mind. Among the other lessons her parents had paid for, she had taken horseback riding. She'd become very proficient at it, but then, it was easy being good at something she enjoyed.

Turning toward Matteo, she told him, "I love horseback riding."

He saw that she meant it. "Good, because we're going on a trail ride."

"Sounds great," she responded with enthusiasm.

What Matteo was proposing was miles away from the kind of date she'd had with Cisco. That evening had been formal, yet flashy. She had no doubt that it cost a pretty penny to dine at that restaurant. But maybe because of how she'd grown up and what she had found out about her father five years ago, flashy made no impression on her whatsoever—except perhaps in a negative way.

So she was relieved and delighted when Matteo brought his car to a stop near a stable and told her that he'd reserved a couple of stallions for them. The horses were both saddled and ready to go.

One had what appeared to be a large wicker basket attached to the saddle horn.

"What's that?" she asked, nodding at the basket.

"That," he told her, "is a surprise. You need any help getting on your horse?" he asked before mounting his.

"Not on your life." She laughed.

As he watched, she mounted her horse in one fluid, graceful movement.

It was like watching poetry in motion, he thought. The line had never meant anything to him before now.

Getting on his horse, Matteo indicated the direction they were about to take. Twilight was still a little more than a hint away.

"Let's go," he told her.

"Does it have anything to do with food?" she teased him, nodding at the basket.

It took him a second to realize what she was referring to. He was far too busy just drinking her in to have room in his thoughts for anything else.

"It might," he finally said. "Play your cards right and you could find out."

In the waning light, she seemed to glow. If he hadn't been half-taken with her already, he would have been now.

Rachel laughed again, the sound wrapping itself around him like a warm embrace. "You're on."

She lost track of time.

They rode their horses along a well-cleared road. It was framed by tall trees on both sides. The sense of peacefulness was irresistible, and she felt both enthusiastic and contented at the same time.

Before she realized it, the sun had completely receded, calling it a day and allowing the full moon to take over.

"Okay, I think it's time to show you that surprise," he said, reining in his horse and dismounting.

She'd almost forgotten about that. "I'm game if you are," she told him, getting off her horse.

Matteo tied his horse's reins to a low-hanging branch on a nearby tree, then took the reins from her horse and did the same.

Rachel wiped her hands on her back pockets and asked, "Need any help?"

He did, Matteo thought, but it wasn't anything that she could help him with. His pulse was just going to have to stop racing on its own.

"No, but thanks for offering," he replied, setting the basket on the ground. He flipped back the top and took out the classic red-checked tablecloth. Two small but bright battery-powered lanterns followed.

As Rachel stood to one side, watching, he went on to get what she thought was a rather impressive picnic dinner for them: fried chicken, biscuits with butter and two servings of fresh fruit. "Dinner is served," he told her.

She didn't sit down at first. Instead, she took it all

in. This, she thought, had taken a lot of effort. When had he had the time to throw it all together? She'd agreed to go out with him only a couple of hours ago.

"Very impressive," she told him. "Where did you fly the chicken in from?" She assumed that was what he'd done since he was a pilot like his father, and making cargo drops appeared to be his main source of income.

You're assuming things again, that little voice in her head chided her.

What he said in response to her question confirmed she was wrong. "I didn't."

"You bought the fried chicken locally," she concluded.

"No," he told her, giving her a coated paper dinner plate that looked prettier than some of the real plates she had seen. "I fried it locally."

Rachel wasn't sure she was following him. "Come again?"

He said it as simply as he could. "I made the chicken."

She looked from the tempting pile of fried chicken pieces to Matteo and then back again. She furrowed her brow in disbelief. "Did you make the biscuits, too?"

His eyes crinkled as he smiled. "Biscuits, too," he repeated.

Her eyes swept over everything one more time. It all looked too perfect. Most men were not this detail-oriented—unless they were professional chefs, and this man was *not* a professional chef.

"You're kidding," she breathed.

Matteo slowly shook his head, then replied, "Not

that I'm aware of." Pausing, he took in her expression. "You look surprised."

"I am," she admitted. "I didn't think that bachelors knew how to cook. Especially city bachelors." Which was what he was, coming from Miami and all, she thought. "It's far too easy to pick up the phone and order takeout than to stand over a hot stove, fooling around with measuring spoons."

"Easy," Matteo agreed. "But doing it that way— calling for takeout—lacks a certain feeling of accomplishment. Although, to be completely honest, I have to admit that I'm a big fan of eating out. They have some truly *amazing* restaurants back in Miami." Temporarily warming to his subject—and recalling favorite meals—he told her with enthusiasm, "Any kind of food you can name, there's a restaurant that specializes in making it.

"I also got to sample my fair share of different kinds of cuisines in some of the cities around the world while I was an airline pilot," he told her, putting a couple of drumsticks on his plate.

She'd thought he just flew cargo. Working for the airlines broadened his base. "Oh, like your Dad."

"Yeah."

Rachel could hear the pride in his voice when he acknowledged that.

"If you like eating out so much," she said, "how did you learn how to cook?" It sounded as if he'd had a busy life. When would he have had the time to take cooking lessons?

"By watching my mom." A fond look slipped over his face. It completely captivated Rachel. "She was an absolutely amazing cook. And she never followed any recipes. She just did everything purely by instinct."

Rachel liked that. Liked the fact that Matteo wasn't embarrassed to learn how to cook or to credit his mother for it. He had no way of knowing that he had just gone up several notches in her book. But he had.

"Is your mother still in Miami?" she asked casually, wondering what the woman was like.

Matteo's face darkened just for an instant before he answered her question. "No. My mother died a few years ago."

She heard the pain in his voice, even though he didn't say anything more on the subject.

"Oh, I'm so sorry, Matteo." Rachel placed her hand over his in a sign of sympathy and comfort. "That must have been so terrible for you and your family."

Taking a deep breath, Matteo shrugged, trying to shed both the feeling and what he assumed was her pity. He didn't want to dwell on the subject any longer.

"Yeah, well, that's all part of life, I guess." And then, just like that, he changed the subject. "I took a chance with the chicken," he admitted. When she looked at him, puzzled, he explained, "Not everybody likes fried chicken."

He had to be hanging around different circles than she did, Rachel thought.

"Well, I never met anyone who didn't like fried chicken. Speaking of which, this has to be just about the very *best* fried chicken I've ever had." It was crisp and golden, light and definitely not greasy—and there was a certain flavor to it that she couldn't put her finger on, but it was very different than the standard fried chicken. She'd bet on it. "What did you use?" she wanted to know.

"I make my own bread crumbs," he admitted.

She stared at him. "God, but you're enterprising." Her bread crumbs came out of a container labeled Seasoned Bread Crumbs.

"It's a secret recipe," he told her, his dark eyes dancing. "But I guess I can trust you. I grind up seasoned garlic croutons, soda crackers and some almonds. Then I mix them all together. Each piece of chicken gets a few drops of extra-virgin olive oil to coat it. Then I dip both sides of the piece in the bread crumbs. After that, the only thing left is the frying." Matteo smiled. "No big deal."

"Well, it tastes like a big deal once it gets to your tongue," she told him. "Your mother would be very proud of you."

The words had no sooner left her mouth than she realized that perhaps he didn't want the conversation to go back in that direction. He had all but closed up a minute ago, right after he had mentioned his mother's passing.

Raising her eyes to his, Rachel glanced at him rather hesitantly. To her relief, rather than looking extremely sad again, Matteo had a small smile on his face. Granted, it was etched with sorrow, but it still qualified as a smile.

"Thanks," he told her. "It means a lot to me to hear that."

Even though he knew Rachel had no idea what his mother would have thought, the idea that his mother would have been proud of him for something so simple as cooking a meal bolstered him.

It occurred to Matteo, as he looked into Rachel's face, that his mother would have liked this woman.

Perhaps even as much as he did.

Chapter Seven

In general, Matteo wasn't a man who was given to impulsive behavior. That was more Cisco's department. For his part, Matteo was a man who thought things out, who weighed things very carefully before making any sort of decision. If Cisco was the fast-moving hare of the famed Aesop's fable, Matteo was the tortoise. Slow and steady, always with his eye on the distant prize.

But just this once, Matteo allowed impulse to rule him. Just this once, he put himself in Cisco's shoes and asked himself what his brother would do in a case like this—*feeling* like this.

Maybe he needed to take a page out of Cisco's book. After all, Cisco was the one who had the girls all clamoring for his attention as far back as Matteo could remember. Cisco was the one who never, *ever* lacked for female companionship.

And Cisco didn't sit around waiting for things to happen. He *made* things happen.

Maybe it was time that he did the same, Matteo thought as desire continued to swirl through him, growing larger and more intense.

With that last thought uppermost in his mind, Matteo cupped Rachel's chin in his hand ever so lightly, tilted her head back and brushed his lips against hers without so much as a whispered preamble or a hint of a warning.

One second they were talking. The next he was seizing the moment and kissing her.

Her lips were incredibly sweet, tasting of the strawberry she had just consumed and her very own unique and tempting flavor. Matteo felt awe and excitement at the same time.

Her scent filled his head, and her taste filled his soul, tempting him. Making him long for things he knew he shouldn't be longing for, not at this point.

It was too soon.

Unlike Cisco, he wasn't the love-'em-and-leave-'em type. That, to him, was the very definition of irresponsibility. To Matteo, family was everything. And he would not accidentally create any new members until after the proper steps had been taken. Caution, he silently argued, could only be thrown to the wind so far before a man's moral fiber wound up being sacrificed.

That wasn't him.

And yet…

And yet she made him ache so badly. Made him want to do and be things that he normally wasn't.

Rachel had to remind herself to breathe.

This was not as good as she thought it might be— it was better.

Miles better.

So much better that she thought perhaps this was what some people referred to when they talked about having an out-of-body experience, because heaven knew, her consciousness had definitely gone *somewhere* these past few minutes.

Without thinking, she wrapped her arms around Matteo's neck, cleaving the upper part of her body to his, her heart racing so madly she thought it might very well burst.

And when it was over, when Matteo pulled his lips from hers, she almost cried out. Part of her wanted to stop him from moving back. She wanted to keep the moment going indefinitely so that she could lose herself in his kiss until both their boundaries were blurred and she didn't know where hers ended and his began.

She felt as if she was free-falling through space.

It wasn't realistic and she knew it, but just for this small interlude of time, she had parted company with reality.

Happily-ever-after fairy tales were more her speed right now.

When he drew his head back, there was an apology automatically hovering on Matteo's lips. But one look at Rachel's face and something told him that it wasn't necessary to apologize. The exact opposite was true. That if he apologized, he would be in effect ruining something perfect.

Something they both treasured in their own unique way.

With effort, Matteo reined in both his thoughts and his growing desires. He told himself he needed to know more about her as a person. This magnetic pull he was experiencing had to have more than just physicality at its core. He wanted to have feelings for the total person, not just the sexy intern/hostess whose presence ignited his soul.

"Does your family live here in Horseback Hollow?" he asked her. Maybe it was a lame question, but it was a start.

The question, coming out of the blue, caught her off guard. Why was he asking that now?

"No, they're back in—someplace else," she ended, deciding at the last moment that it served no purpose to give away too much information.

It wasn't that she didn't trust Matteo or wanted to project the image of some sort of woman of mystery. She just didn't want him to get it in his head to look up her family on one of his piloting jaunts. Who she had been back in Austin was *not* who she was here in Horseback Hollow. She wanted to be judged on her own merits, not on whose daughter she was.

"Why do you ask?" she wanted to know.

His shrug was casual. "Just being curious," he replied. "I have a big family, and we're pretty close. Always makes me wonder what everyone else's family is like."

"My family's big," Rachel acknowledged. "But we're not close," she said flatly, "so it really doesn't count all that much *how* big we are. There were times when we were just ten individuals under the same roof, nothing more."

"Ten, huh?" Matteo whistled at the number. "Well, you've got me beat. I've got only five siblings in mine. But we're all pretty close," he added, wondering if she would take that as a criticism about her family. He certainly didn't mean it that way. "Gabi's the youngest—

and the only girl. When my dad was hurt in that plane crash, Gabi dropped everything and came right out to take care of him. While she was here, she wound up meeting and falling in love with Jude Fortune Jones. After my dad recovered, Gabi got married.

"That's why Cisco and I are out here," he explained. "We came for her wedding."

She liked that about him, liked his family loyalty. She'd been at the wedding, too, but their paths had never crossed. She'd never even caught a glimpse of him. She would have remembered if she had. "She made a beautiful bride, didn't she?"

Matteo nodded. "Yes."

His little sister *had* made a beautiful bride. He couldn't recall ever seeing her glow like that. He was very happy for her. At the same time, he wondered if he was ever going to have that sort of a connection with someone, the kind of connection that felt as if the other person completed him. And he couldn't help but wonder how he and Rachel had spent the night at the same affair without meeting. Without sharing a look or a dance.

Rachel pointed out the obvious. "And you're still here." It gave her an inkling of hope that perhaps he intended to stay around for a while—perhaps even permanently.

Matteo shrugged again, lifting one shoulder carelessly, then letting it drop. "I'm not sure about Cisco's reasons, but as for me, I thought I'd stick around for a little bit just to please the old man. Dad wants all of us to relocate here." He smiled, recalling the blatant hints his father had dropped since he'd arrived in town. It surprised him that Cisco was actually on board with the idea of staying for a while. His brother's primary real-estate market was back in Miami. He would have thought that Cisco would have already been on a plane headed back home. "Dad likes having family close by."

Rachel saw through the layers of rhetoric. "But you want to go back to Miami."

"That was the plan," he admitted, looking up at the sky with its network of stars. If he looked at her, he knew he would be sorely tempted to kiss her again— and this time it might not stop there. So he looked at the sky for both their sakes.

Was. He'd said that "was" the plan, Rachel thought, seizing on the word. Did that mean that there was a new plan in place? Or was she just indulging in a great deal of wishful thinking?

She wasn't sure, and she didn't want to ask Matteo to clarify that for her. He might take her question the wrong way or misunderstand why she was asking.

At this point, even *she* wasn't exactly sure what she meant with all this wavering back and forth she was doing, especially while it was going on with these strange, intense feelings she was having that served as a backdrop for what might or might not be going on between them.

All she knew was that she had never felt so confused before: excited and frightened all at the same time. And it was centered on this man sitting inches away from her.

Rachel pretended to compare the lure of Miami with what Horseback Hollow had to offer. "We don't have the kinds of restaurants or nightlife that Miami boasts," she readily agreed. "But you certainly can't find a more peaceful place than this town." And right now, that was a very high priority for her.

"Assuming I'm looking for peaceful," Matteo pointed out.

"Everyone looks for peaceful once in a while," she told him. And then, thinking it over, she amended her own assessment. "Well, maybe not everyone," she allowed. "Your brother doesn't seem like the type who values peaceful. He seems more like someone who's drawn to nightlife."

He couldn't tell if she was just making an assessment of Cisco—or comparing his brother to him and finding him lacking. Finding him, in a word, dull.

He'd taken second place to his brother more times than he could remember, and while it had only mildly irritated him when he was a boy, this time around, the thought really bothered him.

Matteo began to gather up the dishes and what was left of the picnic, depositing everything rather haphazardly into the basket.

"It's getting late," he announced. "I think I'd better take you home."

She could have sworn she'd seen something flash across his face a moment ago, a thought that didn't sit well with him or some sort of an epiphany that had made him feel less than comfortable.

Whatever it was, it had been abrupt, and she could feel that the mood changed instantly.

Was it something she had unwittingly said? Or done? She didn't have a clue, and it bothered her.

For a moment, Rachel debated just coming out and asking him what was wrong. But that could make things even worse. In the end, she pretended nothing had happened and this was just the natural ending to a moonlight picnic.

As he put away all the plates and utensils, she folded up the tablecloth and handed it to him. She placed the lanterns side by side in the wicker basket.

"Thanks," he murmured, avoiding her eyes.

"Least I can do," she responded. "I really did have a very nice time." She thought perhaps that needed to be reinforced in light of the way their evening had abruptly ended.

For a moment, Matteo stopped moving and packing and looked at her. Was she just being polite while secretly regretting that he wasn't his brother?

Damn it, was he ever going to be rid of this constant feeling of competition, of being measured and rated against his brother— and found lacking? He had his own career, his own way of doing things, his own identity. Why, then, was there always this feeling that he was forever struggling to get out from beneath his brother's long shadow?

"Yeah, me, too," he told her.

His brief acknowledgment coaxed a small smile from her.

It went a long way in warming him up.

Matteo brought her to her apartment door. He wasn't the type just to deposit a woman on her doorstep while he kept his car engine running, ready to make a quick getaway.

He was, however, planning on turning on his heel and leaving as soon as she was safely inside with her door locked.

At least, that had been his initial plan, formed while driving Rachel back.

But as he walked beside her to her door, he felt an

overwhelming desire to linger with her, to say something, *anything*, that didn't brand them as two strangers who happened to have shared an evening meal together, accompanied by an assortment of insects.

He watched as she put her key into the lock and turned it. *Talk now, or forever hold your peace*, he told himself sternly.

Almost to his surprise, he heard himself saying, "Would you mind if I called you sometime? I mean, while I'm still here in Horseback Hollow?"

"You mean you wouldn't fly in from Miami just to see me?" she deadpanned. The next second, she saw the look on his face and realized that he thought she was serious. "I'm kidding," she assured him quickly. "I'm kidding. And no, I wouldn't mind." If ever a man needed a fire lit under him, it was Matteo. "I'd rather like that."

She had surprised him. Matteo was aware of the fact that he hadn't exactly put his best foot forward in the last part of their date. That she was still willing to see him again despite that had him smiling broadly at her. "You would?"

"Uh-huh. Of course, you might have to ply me with more of your fried chicken," she told him.

He looked at her a little uncertainly, as if trying to ascertain whether or not she was pulling his leg.

The man had a lot of good qualities, she thought, but he definitely needed to work on his sense of humor. Someone had forgotten to issue him one.

"Everyone's got a price," she told him, smiling. "Fried chicken is mine. *Your* fried chicken," she emphasized with what was now a wide grin.

Her smile managed to coax a similar one from him. "That can be arranged."

"Good," she said. Had there not been a glimmer in her eyes, he would have been tempted to think that she was serious. Nonetheless, the fact that she had mentioned the main course he'd made for her pleased him.

He knew that he should be leaving. But then, he argued with himself, if for some reason this was the last time they were to be together, it made no sense for him to beat a hasty retreat, especially since she wasn't the one who was trying to get him to leave.

Searching for something to say, he fell back on work. That was always a reliable topic, and right now, it was probably also a necessary one.

"You, um, might want to tell your boss to clear some more space in one of the smaller rooms in your building. Dad told me that there're going to be several more deliveries made to your branch of the Fortune Foundation this month. We're going to be flying between Red Rock and Horseback Hollow at least three more times."

She couldn't begin to imagine what they would be flying out on three more trips—even as she was doing a little happy dance in her head. Three more trips meant seeing Matteo at least three more times— at the very least.

She knew it took a lot of supplies to start up a large office and run it efficiently. There were still offices that were essentially empty within the two-story building. She imagined that Matteo and his father might even be flying in the furniture for those offices, among other things.

"I guess that means we'll be getting more than

just printer paper and ink cartridges delivered," Rachel said.

Matteo laughed. He'd seen the pages upon pages of inventory regarding the cargo being shipped to the Horseback Hollow branch office.

"Way more," he agreed.

"Are you going to be the one delivering those deliveries? Does your dad agree to having you pilot the cargo plane instead of him?" she asked.

Having opened the door to her apartment, she now leaned against the door frame, reluctant to cross the threshold and thereby officially call an end to their date.

"Delivering those deliveries," he echoed, then grinned. "Say that three times, fast."

Rachel felt her heart flutter. She could so easily get lost in that appealing grin of his.

"My tongue doesn't tangle, if that's what you're indirectly asking about." Then, to prove it, she repeated the sentence three times, enunciating each word quickly and clearly. "Anything else you'd like to hear me recite?" she asked.

He could have sworn there was mischief in her eyes. This was a woman who everyone thought was relatively quiet, but who, in reality, was a live wire who seemed capable of doing anything on a whim, then resuming looking angelic.

He wasn't sure which one attracted him more, the angel or the devil.

Most likely, he thought, it was a mixture of both. But he didn't want to waste whatever precious moments there were left before she retreated into her apartment and he drove back to his father's house.

He had his suspicions that dreams of Miami weren't going to be nearly as strong and alluring tonight as they had been of late.

"I just wanted to tell you one more time that I had a very nice time tonight," he said.

She surprised him—and herself—by saying, "Show me."

Matteo looked at her, confused. "What?"

"Show me," Rachel repeated.

"How?" he asked, not exactly sure he understood what she was getting at.

Her mouth curved, underscoring the amusement that was already evident in her eyes.

"Oh, I think you can figure it out, Mendoza," she told him. Then she sighed loudly, took hold of the two sides of his button-down shirt and abruptly pulled him to her.

Matteo was more than a little surprised at this display of proactive behavior on her part. She really was a firecracker, he thought.

The next moment, there was no room for looks of surprise or any other expressions, for that matter. It was hard to make out a woman's features if her face was flush against another face the way Rachel's was against his.

She lost no time in putting a piece of her soul into the kiss. If the first kiss between them during the picnic was sweet, this kiss was nothing if not flaming hot. So much so that Matteo was almost certain he was going to go up in smoke any second now.

The thing of it was, he didn't care. As long as it happened while he was kissing Rachel, nothing else mattered.

Chapter Eight

"I'd better leave now, while I still can," Matteo told her a full two minutes later, separating himself from her.

He knew he had to pull back, and it had to be *now*. He had a very strong feeling that, despite any noble sentiments to the contrary, if he waited even a single moment longer, he would be completely lost. A man could resist only so much temptation before he gave in, and in all honesty, he wasn't altogether sure that things were happening for the right reasons.

Did this woman make his blood surge because he was so attracted to her, or was it because somewhere, deep down, he felt his brother was interested in Rachel, and he was trying to best Cisco at his own game?

If it was the latter, then going any further tonight would be a complete disservice to her, not to mention wrong.

And she deserved better than that. Better than to be the object of a tug-of-war between two brothers.

Rachel looked somewhat dazed and sounded a bit breathless when she said, "You're being a gentleman."

Matteo wasn't sure if she was making an assessment or asking him a question. In either case, the answer was the same. He was taking no credit for something that was not a done deal.

"I'm trying."

Rachel smiled up into his eyes, both disappointed and absolutely thrilled and touched.

"I appreciate that," she whispered.

And even though she truly wanted to make love with him, she had to admire his restrained behavior. Not every man was like that, holding back until they had spent more time together.

"Then, like I said, I'd better leave now." Matteo took a step back, away from her door. His eyes never left her face. "I'll see you soon," he promised.

She had no doubt that she would see him again. But in what capacity? "Professionally or privately?" Rachel asked.

Matteo merely smiled enigmatically at her and said, "Yes."

Turning from Rachel, he began to walk away. As he left, he heard her cell phone begin to ring. In his gut, he knew who it was.

Cisco.

Stiffening, he slowed his pace, wanting to see if he was right. He had no idea how he knew who was calling her. He just did.

Confirmation came as he listened to her end of the

conversation. He could feel his gut twisting. Maybe he *should* have let things progress naturally.

Every word she uttered pierced his skin like tiny blades.

"Oh, it's you. No, just surprised, that's all. Yes, I just got in. Very nice, thank you."

Matteo resisted the temptation of pulling the cell out of her hand and telling his brother where he could go. Gritting his teeth, he kept walking.

By the time he got to his car, Matteo had sufficiently worked himself up. Looking down at his sides, Matteo realized that both his hands were clenched.

Had Cisco been standing in front of him right now, he wouldn't have been standing upright for long.

The following morning found him sitting across from Cisco, having breakfast at a cafe in Vicker's Corners. The arrangements to meet had been made a week ago, to discuss their father's situation without having their father present. But at the moment, the subject of their father was the furthest thing from either of their minds.

Cisco was consuming his breakfast as if he didn't have a care in the world. No such laid-back attitude resided on Matteo's side of the table. Matteo had come because he had given his word, but he was not happy about having to be in such proximity to his brother, who was, for the most part, acting even more cocky than usual, in his estimation.

Cisco seemed to be scrutinizing him. Why? What was going on in his brother's head? Matteo couldn't help wondering.

"I hear your date went well last night," Cisco told

him, nodding his head in approval. "A moonlight picnic. You're improving, little brother. There's hope for you yet."

Matteo didn't like Cisco's blatantly high-handed attitude, nor did he like the fact that his brother was prying into his personal life as if he had every right to. He saw it as nothing less than an invasion of privacy.

"What business is any of this of yours?" Matteo wanted to know. He angrily swished his fork through the eggs on his plate. If they hadn't been scrambled already, they would have been now.

Scrambled, but not touched.

That was not the case with Cisco's order. His breakfast was disappearing quickly. "Why, you wound me, Mattie." He pressed his hand dramatically against his chest, in the general vicinity of his heart. "Everything about you is my business. If I don't look after you, who will?" he asked loftily.

Matteo narrowed his eyes. "I don't need looking after," he snapped.

"That is a matter of opinion," Cisco replied, amused. Pausing, holding his fork aloft, he asked, "Have you asked her out again?"

Matteo's eyes narrowed. "Asked who out again?"

Cisco shook his head. He made it obvious that this kind of a response was definitely beneath his brother. "Oh, don't play dumb, Mattie. We both know you're not dumb. You might lack energy and drive, and God knows you're slow to pick up on signals—"

Matteo was trying to ignore his brother, but Cisco was making it next to impossible. "*What* signals?" he demanded.

Cisco used his fork as if it was an extension of

his hand, waving it at his brother as he spoke. "See, that's my point exactly. You don't even know there *are* any signals. Since I'm your older brother and I believe in leading by example, if you don't take advantage of what's right there in front of you, then I'm going to have to step in and do it for you—for your own good, of course."

Now, what was *that* supposed to mean?

A waitress approached their table at that moment, a coffeepot in her hand. She topped off Cisco's coffee with more than half a cup.

There was hardly room for a drop more in Matteo's cup. It was obvious that he hadn't touched any of his breakfast.

"Is everything all right with your meal, sir?" the young woman asked.

"My *meal* is fine," he told her. His eyes never left his brother.

The waitress, looking somewhat confused, withdrew.

The moment she did, Matteo asked his brother incredulously, "You're putting me on notice?"

"I suppose that's one way of saying it," Cisco allowed. "Bottom line is that we can't have Rachel thinking all the Mendoza men are slow to act just because you are."

He could see that Cisco was enjoying this exchange. He, on the other hand, definitely was not.

"Stay away from her," Matteo warned his brother, his voice low, foreboding.

Everything about Cisco's body language told Matteo that his older brother was not about to follow instructions.

"I'm afraid I can't do that," Cisco said. "This is a free country, little brother, and the last time I looked, there weren't any 'taken' signs on Rachel."

If they hadn't been sitting in a public place, Matteo would have been sorely tempted to wipe the smirk off his brother's all-too-handsome face. "Then use your imagination," he growled.

"Oh, I am," Cisco assured him with a hearty laugh. "I am."

At this point, goaded this way, it took every last drop of restraint that Matteo possessed to keep him from jumping up from the table and making his brother eat his words.

Maybe he wouldn't have succeeded—Cisco wasn't exactly a ninety-pound weakling; he was a man who believed in exercising to keep physically fit—but Matteo would have gotten a great deal of satisfaction out of trying and landing at least a couple of well-placed punches.

But he refrained from any sort of physical action because he knew that if word got back to his father— and it would—that he and Cisco were publicly brawling, it would really upset the old man. Not because it happened in public, but that it happened at all.

His father was very big on family unity. Trying to beat each other up didn't exactly strike a blow for family unity. It just struck a blow.

But if he couldn't vent his anger via his method of choice, at least he didn't have to remain here, listening to Cisco talk as if he was the leading authority on women and relationships.

Standing up, Matteo threw a couple of bills on the table.

"Where are you going?" Cisco asked innocently. He indicated Matteo's plate. "You haven't finished your breakfast yet."

"Oh, I'm finished with it, all right," Matteo retorted. "Besides, I suddenly lost my appetite."

Cisco nodded as if he had been expecting to hear that. "Unresolved love issues can do that to a man."

Didn't Cisco ever stop pontificating? Or, at the very least, get sick of the sound of his own voice?

"I don't have time to listen to you babble. I've got work to do," Matteo said, turning on his heel and walking away.

Cisco leaned back in his chair, tilting it slightly so he could get a better view of his brother as he left the restaurant.

"If that means making deliveries to a certain charitable foundation, say hi to her for me," Cisco called after him.

Matteo bit his tongue. Answering his brother would only lead to yet another round of exchanges that went nowhere. Cisco was not one to surrender his right to get in the last word—*each time*. Matteo had no doubt that his brother would probably go on talking from the grave if it seemed as if someone got in the last word after him.

Besides, the truth of it was, he really did have to hustle. His father *was* making another round-trip run today to the Fortune Foundation's headquarters in Red Rock and back again.

He knew for a fact that his father would take off without him if he wasn't there on time. While Orlando Mendoza made it known that he enjoyed all his children's company, he also made it known that it irked him no end to have anyone think he needed a keeper or someone watching over him, ready to step in at the first sign of any sort of weakness.

Matteo supposed, as the comparison snuck up on him, that his father felt the same way about his being around for the flights as he himself felt hearing Cisco tell him that he was willing to lead by example.

"But it's different," he said out loud, as if he was making the argument to his father instead of just talking to himself as he drove to the airfield. "If something goes wrong or I don't act fast enough, I'm not going to crash and burn."

And neither was his father. Not if he had anything to say about it.

Which was why he needed to get to the airfield right now. He wanted to check out the plane himself despite the fact that the Redmond Flight School and Charter Service kept a very reliable mechanic on its payroll.

"I was just about to leave without you," Orlando told him as Matteo raced onto the field, having parked his vehicle as close as was allowed. "I thought perhaps your date with that cute girl went well, so you weren't going to be my shadow anymore now that you found something better to do with your time."

"Nothing's better than working with you, Dad," Matteo told him, forcing a cheerful smile onto his face. "Was your plane checked out?"

"Yes, *hijo*," Orlando said patiently, rolling his eyes heavenward as if he resented being treated like a man who had been born without common sense, "my plane has been checked out. Why aren't you with that girl?

The one from the Foundation—Rachel?" he wanted to know. "Didn't the two of you go out last night?"

Did *everyone* know his business? Matteo wondered. "How did you know about that?" he asked, doing his best not to show that having his personal life viewed as something on public record was extremely irritating to him.

"I'm a father," Orlando told him matter-of-factly. Matteo knew that he was not above doing a little snooping or information swapping to keep an eye on his sons. "Fathers know these things." And then he asked, concerned, "Didn't it go well?"

Since they were flying an empty plane, there was no reason for any further delay once they were on board. "Yes, Dad, it went well."

"Then what are you doing here?" his father wanted to know as he got on the plane. "Why aren't you having breakfast or whatever with her?"

Matteo followed his father onto the plane, entering the cockpit right after he did. "Because she's working at the Foundation this morning, and I'm working here with you. And, according to the timetable you showed me, we're falling behind," he pointed out. "So let's get going."

Orlando, strapping himself into his seat, paused for a moment to look sharply at his youngest son. "Has anyone ever told you that you nag?"

Matteo grinned cheerfully. "Not lately, Dad."

Orlando snorted. Putting on the glasses that he was too vain to wear in public, he looked over his manifest. "Well, you do."

"Must run in the family," Matteo said, staring at his father pointedly.

Orlando ignored him.

"Hey, Dad?"

Orlando glanced in his direction. "Now what?"

"How do you know if a woman's right for you? If she's 'the one'?"

"She tells you," Orlando said as he went over his controls.

"No, really. I'm serious."

"So was I." But because he saw that his son was actually waiting for him to say something, Orlando told him the only thing he could. "Something in your soul connects with hers, perhaps just for a second, and that feeling is so wonderful you just *know* you were meant to be together."

"Was it like that for you and Mom?" Matteo wanted to know.

After a moment, Orlando replied quietly, "Yes."

Matteo knew better than to take the discussion any further.

She was too old for this, Rachel thought a little more than two weeks later as she sat in her cubicle at the Foundation.

Too old to be behaving like a schoolgirl.

Yet no matter where she was, whether working her part-time job at the Cantina or her full-time job here at the Foundation, every time she heard an outer door open or glimpsed someone coming in out of the corner of her eye, before she could make out who it was, her heart was already skipping a beat in hopeful anticipation.

She would have thought, after having gone out with Matteo several times now, to the movies in Vicker's

Corners, for another picnic and to the fancy restaurant where Cisco had initially brought her—which seemed so much more special with Matteo—that she would have gotten a little calmer about the whole thing. Instead, the exact opposite seemed to be true. Each time they went out, she grew more excited about seeing him. It didn't matter what they were doing; it just mattered that she was doing it with him.

Rachel thought back to the last date they'd had and she smiled, reliving it.

"That was really good," she recalled commenting as they left the restaurant in Vicker's Corners. "Not as good as the fried chicken *you* made, of course," she'd amended, a smile playing on her lips, "but still good."

"Yeah, yeah." Matteo had laughed and taken her hand in his. "Feel like going for a little walk before we drive back to Horseback Hollow?"

She'd inclined her head, pretending to think it over, then said, "I'm game." And she was. Game for anything that allowed her to have a little more time with the man she was developing deep feelings for.

"That's one of the things I like about you," he'd told her. "You're game, but you don't play games. Other women think that keeping secrets and being hard to read makes them more desirable to a guy. But with you, I know that what I see is what I get. No games, no mysteries, just total honesty." He'd squeezed her hand affectionately. "That's a rare trait."

She'd frozen then, although she'd tried not to. But the very thing that he'd professed to like best about her wasn't true. She wasn't being up-front and honest with him. In that case, she was being the exact opposite.

She'd felt like a liar—and yet, she couldn't tell him

about her father, about her. Not yet. Not until she felt confident enough about their relationship, about him, to trust him with her story. This wasn't some tiny, inconsequential thing. To her this was a major secret.

She'd stopped walking. "You know, it's getting late. Maybe I should be getting back."

He'd looked at her, undoubtedly surprised by the sudden change in her demeanor. What he'd said next confirmed it for her.

"Did I say something wrong, Rachel?"

"No, no," she'd adamantly denied. "I just forgot that I promised Christopher I'd look into something for him before tomorrow morning. Sorry. I did have a lovely time," she had emphasized.

For a second, he'd looked uncertain—and then he'd grinned. "Come on, Cinderella," he teased. "I'll get you home before you turn into a pumpkin."

"It's the coach that turned into a pumpkin." She laughed, relieved that he wasn't making a big deal out of her sudden reversal.

"Whatever," he'd said good-naturedly.

And that was that. Or so she fervently hoped— although she had caught him looking at her a couple of times as if he knew she was holding something back.

But then again, that could have just been her guilty conscience and her imagination.

It still didn't change anything about the way she felt about him. If anything, since he didn't grill her, it just made her more attracted to him.

And anticipate his appearance each time anyone came into the office or the Cantina. And most of the time, she was disappointed. It was only someone else coming in.

But then again, there was that handful of times when she wasn't disappointed.

That handful of times she and her skipping heartbeat were right.

Those were the times Matteo and his father came walking in, a clipboard in Matteo's hand with a receipt for her to sign in acknowledgment of that day's incoming shipment.

Those were the times that all was right with the world—and her heart.

Thanks to Matteo and his father, the Foundation's offices were taking shape, becoming close to fully operational.

And, also thanks to Matteo, so was their relationship.

Oh, it wasn't progressing by leaps and bounds by any means. Theirs was more of a work in progress, moving along by inches, not feet. But every inch gained was a strong inch, an inch that wouldn't give way or break under its own weight.

Anything worthwhile took time to build. Wasn't that something her father had once said to her back when she thought that the sun rose and set around the man?

Just because everything she had known about her father had turned out to be a lie didn't mean that everything he'd said had been a lie, as well.

There had been *some* truthful things that had come out of his mouth. She had to try to remember that, Rachel told herself.

As she sat at her desk this bright, sunny March day, her mind wandering rather than focusing on the work she had pulled up on her computer monitor, Rachel couldn't help wondering what her father would have thought of Matteo Mendoza.

The very next moment, as if coming to, she abruptly shut that thought away.

It didn't matter to her what her father thought about anything, she upbraided herself. Especially not about the man who had so easily found his way into her heart.

Her father had had a place in her heart, and he'd just thrown that away because of all of his lies.

Because of who—and what—he had finally admitted to being. As far as she knew, she was the *only* one who knew about his secret, but that didn't make her feel privileged.

It made her feel ill.

What would Matteo say if he knew her father was a philanderer, a liar?

Rachel looked up at the clock on the wall. It was getting close to two o'clock.

She could feel her spirits beginning to sink lower. If Matteo and his father had been coming in today, they would have already been here by now, she thought. She'd made a mental note each time the two men came in with a shipment of supplies. The times varied, but they'd never arrived this late.

Apparently, today wasn't a day that they would be dropping off anything at the Foundation, she concluded.

Rachel did her best not to show her disappointment.

"You haven't been to lunch yet," Christopher said as he stopped by her cubicle on his way to his own office.

She was surprised that her boss had noticed. She thought of him as being too busy to notice minor details like that.

"I'm not very hungry," she confessed, then added, "Too much coffee, I guess," in case he was going to comment on the possible reason behind her loss of appetite. The last thing she wanted was to have anyone here speculating about Matteo and her.

"Well, take a break at least. I don't want people thinking I'm working my interns to death," Christopher said. He was smiling, but she could tell that he was serious.

Just then, they heard a commotion in the hall. Though she tried to disguise her reaction, she felt her face light up instantly. She was more than familiar with that particular noise by now. The Foundation's dolly had one squeaky wheel.

Apparently it wasn't as late as she had thought. Matteo and his father had arrived with their latest shipment of goods for the Foundation.

She sat up at attention, ready to be of assistance. It didn't go unnoticed.

"Appetite suddenly reappear?" Christopher asked her, amusement highlighting his handsome features.

"I think that maybe I could eat something after all," Rachel answered evasively.

Although she had a feeling that there really was no point in pretending indifference to Matteo's arrival. It seemed as if everyone on staff here was aware of her feelings for Matteo Mendoza.

Everyone, that was, but Matteo himself. He seemed to be rather oblivious to it. But some men, she knew, took a while to come around, and that was fine with her. She was in no particular hurry.

The next minute, Matteo came into the office, pushing the dolly before him, a very low recurring squeak accompanying his route. The dolly was loaded down with all manner of supplies, including a good month's worth of coffee, the kind that needed to be brewed.

Apparently Christopher knew how to treat his people, Rachel thought absently. The bulk of her attention was otherwise focused.

The moment she made eye contact with Matteo, she automatically began to smile broadly.

Matteo's expression, however, was far more in keeping with being grim.

The next minute she saw why.

His father, being the pilot of record, had of course made the round-trip from here to Red Rock and back with him. But there was also someone else who had come in with them.

Cisco.

Chapter Nine

Circumventing both his father and his younger brother, Cisco headed straight for Rachel the second he walked into the room.

"Hello." Greeting her warmly, he took her hands between his and held them for what seemed to Matteo to be an overly long period. "I see you're looking just as lovely as ever." He spared Matteo the most fleeting of glances before turning his attention back to Rachel. "I guess my brother's efforts to show you a good time have been at least moderately successful."

As gracefully as possible, she extracted her hands from Cisco's. To say that his appearance here surprised her would have been a huge understatement. It also made her somewhat uncomfortable. She had thought that the notion of the two brothers engaged in a competition was a thing of the past. Now she wasn't really all that sure that it was.

"Cisco, I didn't expect to see you here."

The smile Cisco flashed at her widened. "I came to lend my father and little brother a hand—and, of course, to see you again," he told her with what sounded like sincerity.

He moved to take her hands in his again, but she outmaneuvered him, picking up a clipboard from her desk and holding on to it with both hands.

"It hasn't been that long since we saw each other," she pointed out. Her smile felt tense around the edges. She slanted a quick glance in Matteo's direction to see how he was dealing with all this, but his expression was unreadable—and stoic.

"Well, it certainly feels that way to me," Cisco confided. Once again, he glanced over his shoulder toward his brother. "But I didn't want to intrude or steal my brother's thunder, such as it is."

She could feel a blush coming on. It was a direct result of her embarrassment and the flustered feeling that was growing more intense by the second. She had no idea why Cisco was paying this amount of attention to her—they had had a nice date that one time, but it couldn't have been considered spectacular by any means. And the important thing was that Cisco hadn't followed up on it—other than that first time when Matteo had grabbed her cell phone from her and said that he was her date that night.

On the other hand, she and Matteo had had several dates now, and in her opinion, the two of them seemed to be getting closer.

Until today.

If she were to go only by the expression on Matteo's face, she would have said that they did *not* have *any* sort of a relationship at all. He looked distant and removed.

Feeling somewhat frustrated, Rachel turned toward Orlando, hoping to uncover a bit of sanity there. The senior Mendoza had behaved as if he liked her, and she gravitated toward that now.

"What are you delivering today, Mr. Mendoza?" she asked, moving closer to the older man and completely ignoring the other two men for the moment.

"The tables and chairs for the main break room," he told her. "As well as some small appliances. Besides this mini refrigerator, there are a couple of microwaves in the truck." He nodded at Cisco. "Cisco volunteered to help get them off the truck and bring them up in the elevator, putting them where they belonged."

"We're bringing in a couple of vending machines, too," Cisco told her. "Can't have my father and my little brother straining their backs with all this heavy lifting."

Pivoting the dolly so that they could bring it and what was on it to the proper place, Matteo snapped between clenched teeth, "Stop calling me that."

Cisco positioned himself on the dolly's other side. Industrial-size bungee cords were in place to keep the mini refrigerator from moving around in transit, but it seemed that they still needed someone or something to stabilize the appliance's weight. That was Cisco's part in all this.

"Calling you what?" Cisco asked his brother in an innocent voice.

Matteo blew out a breath. Cisco knew exactly what

he was referring to. Why was he pretending not to? "Your little brother."

Cisco's innocent expression never wavered. "Well, you are, aren't you?"

Not knowing how else to deal with this tense situation—and afraid it might get worse any second—Rachel decided to make light of it, desperately hoping to change the mood for the better.

She turned toward their father and asked, "Were they always like this?"

"No," Orlando replied in all seriousness. "They were much worse." Rachel didn't know if she quite believed that was possible. "I think," Orlando went on, "they're on their good behavior because of you."

As if to reinforce his father's statement, Cisco offered her a wide, wide smile. It was obviously forced, yet somehow still rather appealing.

Only Matteo remained silent, applying himself instead to bringing the mini refrigerator they had on the dolly to the appropriate place.

Unaware of the location of the official break room that they were charged with setting up, Matteo looked at Rachel and, nodding at the dolly, asked, "Where do you want this?"

"You mean she has to direct you around the office?" Cisco marveled, chuckling to himself. He looked at Rachel. "I've got to say, Rachel, not every woman would be so patient."

Matteo had had just about all he could take. Ordinarily, what Cisco said when he got on this leader-of-the-pack kick went in one ear and out the other. But this time it was different. This time there was more at stake than just his ego.

"You want to step outside?" Matteo challenged his brother.

"Later," Cisco replied calmly, as if they were having an actual discussion, "to get the next load after we put this one wherever it's supposed to go."

Matteo's eyes narrowed. "That's not what I meant," he said under his breath, only loud enough for his brother to hear.

"But that's what you should have meant," Cisco answered cheerfully, as if he were the soul of reason and hadn't a clue what was bothering Matteo. "You coming?" he asked as he nodded toward the break room. "Or are you saving your back for a rainy day?"

At that precise moment, Matteo could have strangled him—but there were far too many witnesses around. Instead, he pushed the dolly down the hall, his biceps straining and displaying an impressive network of definition.

The view wasn't lost on Rachel.

It went like that for most of the delivery. Barbs between the brothers were exchanged, fast and furiously at every available opportunity. It continued even though Orlando had upbraided both his sons, taking advantage of Rachel stepping out of the room.

He knew that Matteo would take Cisco's ribbing only so long and then he'd come back giving as good—or better—than he got. He didn't want this growing conflict to get out of hand—and he didn't care for the fact that it was on display where someone outside the family could be privy to it.

Especially the woman who was apparently at the center of the reason for this conflict.

"What has gotten into you?" Orlando demanded of Cisco, drawing him over to one side.

"Just making sure that little brother makes the most of his opportunities."

Confused, Orlando stared at his older son. "Really? Well, from here it looks like you are doing your best to undermine Matteo and run him into the ground right in front of that young woman."

"You are right, Dad," Cisco agreed, stunning his father with what seemed like an admission. "It looks that way. But it's not."

Walking into the break room, Cisco frowned at the mini refrigerator that he and Matteo had brought up earlier. He turned to his father and said, "Someone's going to have to call a plumber to hook this baby up if they want it up and running when they finally open their doors to the public in April."

Matteo paused to look at the connections and the capped-off copper tubing. "They don't need a plumber," he told his father. "I can hook this up. I've got a toolbox in your truck." Passing his father, he promised, "Be right back."

"You are a handy little guy to have around, aren't you?" Cisco proclaimed with a laugh.

Matteo stopped for a second right next to his brother. "You call me little one more time and it's not my handy side that you'll be seeing."

Cisco looked amused to have riled his younger brother to this point. "Tempting as that might be to witness, I will do my best to curb my desire to refer to you as little," Cisco told him.

Matteo made no reply as he left the room and took

the stairs to the ground floor. He apparently needed to blow off some steam.

Neither brother realized that they were being watched and that Rachel had heard the entire exchange between them.

Because the physical preparation of the Foundation's offices were part of her duties, Rachel made herself accessible the entire time the Mendozas were at the Foundation. It didn't matter whether they were unloading the truck or bringing up the various pieces of furniture and appliances. She made sure that she was right there, ready to help in any way that was necessary.

Unlike the previous occasions when Matteo and his father made deliveries, with Cisco present, Matteo didn't do much talking. Because Rachel didn't want to get in the middle of whatever was going on between the two brothers, she found herself doing a great deal of talking to their father.

The senior Mendoza was a strikingly handsome man who was every bit as charming as Cisco and just as warm and genuine as Matteo. As she spoke to the man, discussing work and his family, she delicately inquired how he was getting along on his own after having been married for so long.

Orlando took a moment to frame his reply.

"I am not surprised that you know," he told her. "You strike me as a very intelligent young lady who makes a point of looking into people's backgrounds if you are going to be dealing with them on any sort of a long-term basis."

He had her pegged, she thought. At least, he had

the old Rachel pegged. The one who had yet to be blown out of the water by her own father. Reconstructing a life wasn't easy after discovering that the person you thought you knew was a complete and total stranger to you—like her father was to her.

The worst part of it, she thought now, was that she *hadn't* actually been able to confront her father about her discovery. She had found it easier to leave home, spouting some nonsense about finding herself.

But for right now, she was focusing on Orlando. "You didn't answer my question," she pointed out gently.

"No, I didn't," Orlando agreed. Then, because he knew she meant well and wasn't being nosy, he told her, "I'm getting along as well as possible, seeing as how she was the light of my soul and she was taken from me much too early." With a vague little shrug, Orlando went on to say, "I miss her every day. I suspect I will until the day I die."

"You should try going out," Rachel suggested sympathetically.

He looked at her as if she had suggested that he run naked through traffic at twilight.

"From what you told me, your wife sounds like she was a lovely lady who wouldn't have wanted you to go on grieving for her endlessly. She'd want you to go out, to have a good time and to meet other people."

The idea of putting himself out there after all these years was not an appealing one. "No, I think that, at least for now, I should remain on the sidelines. I have plenty to keep me occupied," he added quickly, building up his excuses so that this young woman would refrain from the idea of playing matchmaker in case that was her inclination. "There is my job, flying cargo to various places, not to mention playing referee between my two sons. Although, I must say, I can see why they would be butting heads over you."

She could feel her cheeks reddening again. "Now, don't you start," Rachel warned him, half kidding. He was, after all, a Mendoza, and his sons had to get their flirtatious personas from somewhere. Orlando raised his hands as if in surrender. "I only made an observation. After all, I am not blind, and even I can see how very lovely you are."

Laughing, she shook her head. "I can see that Cisco inherited his silver tongue from you."

Orlando dramatically placed his hand over his heart. "Please, senorita, you make me blush."

"Not hardly, Senor Mendoza," she responded, looking at him knowingly. "Not hardly."

Matteo and Cisco worked hard to set up the break room. Even so, Cisco made sure that he had time to interact with Rachel several times during the length of their workday—and always in full view of Matteo. The latter seemed determined to continue working nonstop—especially when Rachel tried to talk to him. She made three attempts at having a conversation with Matteo, but each time, he made it clear that he was busy with some other part of the shipment, unable—and possibly unwilling—to take the time to stop and talk with her.

By the time the three men were ready to leave, she was more than willing to see them go. At least when it came to Matteo. His deliberate inattention toward her had stung.

Picking up on the tension that was humming between the duo, Cisco leaned in and told her— quite audibly—"Don't worry. He'll get over it."

Whatever "it" was, she thought.

"I'm not worried and I really don't care," she informed Cisco with a toss of her head. She made a point of completely ignoring Matteo, acting as if he wasn't even there. After all, a woman had her pride, Rachel thought. Without it, she was nothing, and she for one was determined never to feel that way, not even for five minutes.

"See you around, beautiful," Cisco said cheerfully by way of parting.

"See you around," she echoed, holding on to the receipt that Orlando had given her for that day's deliveries.

Orlando hung behind and gave her a courtly bow. "Thank you for everything—and I do apologize for my sons," he emphasized again.

"You have only one to apologize for," Rachel pointed out. "The other one—Cisco—" she added in case there was any doubt "—was very charming."

It was obvious that Orlando had another opinion on the matter, but he didn't contradict her. Instead, he said, "Perhaps that is why I need to apologize— for the other one," he emphasized. "Do not write him off too quickly, please."

Maybe there was a misunderstanding about all this, she thought. "I'm not looking for anything right now, Senor Mendoza."

Orlando gave her another small, courtly bow. "Understood," he told her.

He withdrew from the room and then from the

building. Both of his sons were waiting in the truck. He intended to give one of them hell, but not necessarily the one that Rachel had assumed would be on the receiving end.

"Idiot!"

The word echoed around her apartment—not for the first time.

Rachel called herself a fool for caring about Matteo. She knew she should consider herself lucky that she had been made privy to his sullen side before things had really heated up between them.

It would have been so much worse if she had fallen in love with him, she thought, roaming around her ground-floor apartment like a caged tiger, unable to find a place for herself. Everywhere she sat down felt all wrong. *She* felt all wrong.

She'd never felt this restless before.

And he had done that to her, she thought angrily. Matteo Mendoza had taken her goodwill and her affections and made mincemeat out of them, treating her like less than a stranger just because his brother had flirted with her. She certainly hadn't done anything to encourage Cisco.

Was Matteo afraid she would become enamored with the flirtatious words his brother was spouting? Did he really think so little of her that he assumed she'd just fall all over herself if his brother flashed a sexy smile at her and acted as if he was interested?

And why was she wasting time sulking about Matteo when she should be purging all thoughts of him out of her head? She hadn't done anything wrong and Matteo had barely talked to her today.

As a matter of fact, he *hadn't* talked to her. He'd just grunted and uttered single-word sentences. Well, that wasn't going to fly, not where she was concerned.

Rachel looked around her apartment. Suddenly it felt too small to her. She felt trapped, as if she needed to get out.

But where and with whom?

She hadn't made too many close friends here aside from Shannon—who was now occupied with her new family-to-be—and that was her own fault. She'd been leery of getting hurt again. Her father, she thought not for the first time, had done some number on her.

What she needed to do was swear off any contact with men whatsoever, young *or* old.

Right now, that didn't seem like a hard thing to do.

When the doorbell rang, it caught her completely by surprise. She wasn't expecting anyone, and she didn't know anyone who was prone to paying visits at the drop of a hat.

When the doorbell rang again, she came to the conclusion that whoever was on the other side of the door was not about to go home until she gave the order. And right now, she was angry enough to do exactly that.

Swinging the door open, she shouted, "Go away!" just as she came face-to-face with her uninvited guest.

And found herself looking at Matteo.

Chapter Ten

For a second, she could only stare at him.

"Matteo, what are you doing here?" Rachel finally managed to ask. He was the very *last* person she would have expected to turn up on her doorstep tonight.

Or, considering today's display at the Foundation, ever.

All the way over to her apartment, Matteo tried to talk himself out of coming to see her. At each corner, he told himself to turn the car around and go back. If he went through with this, he was only setting himself up for a fall. Rachel was going to break his heart. He was sure of it.

Coming here tonight, feeling the way he did, was *not* a good idea, he muttered to himself as he drove.

Yet somehow he couldn't get himself to turn

around, couldn't make himself pull over and rethink his next move.

Carefully.

It was as if he was on automatic pilot and had no real say or control over what he was about to do.

Though he was afraid of what he would see, Matteo looked over Rachel's shoulder into her apartment—or what he could see of it.

"Am I interrupting anything?" he asked her, his voice low, bordering on an accusation.

"Yes, you're interrupting something," she informed him, her hands on her hips and her eyebrows furrowing. "You're interrupting my efforts to secure some peace and quiet, which, after the kind of day I just had, would be desperately appreciated."

"You're sure that's all I'm interrupting?" Matteo asked pointedly.

Granted, he hadn't seen Cisco's car when he'd driven up, but that didn't mean it wasn't parked somewhere on the other side of the small apartment complex. And it certainly didn't mean that his brother wasn't here, perhaps even in her bedroom, waiting for him to leave.

Matteo looked at her, his sensitive face dark, his eyes pinning her in place. "I'm not interrupting your date?"

"What date?" she demanded. She was getting really angry at his attitude, and she was more than a little insulted.

He'd gone this far. He might as well spit out the rest of it, even though something within him wanted him to retreat. "With Cisco."

Rachel tossed her head, struggling to contain her anger.

"I *have* no date with Cisco," she informed Matteo coldly. "If I did, I wouldn't try to hide it. But I don't. So now you have your answer, and you can go back to wherever it was you came from."

Angry, hurt, insulted, Rachel started to slam the door on him, but Matteo put his hand up against it. He was a great deal stronger than she was, and he kept the door exactly where it was.

Exasperated, Rachel cried, "What do you want from me?"

Had he cared about her less, he would have behaved more rationally. But this was brand-new territory for him, and he was having trouble finding his way.

No more games, he told himself. *Just the truth.* "I came to ask you a question."

She could see that she wasn't going to be rid of Matteo until he got this—whatever *this* was—off his chest. She resigned herself to hearing him out.

"All right, ask your question. The sooner you ask, the sooner you can go away," she retorted.

He was putting himself out on a limb, hanging fifty feet above the ground, vulnerable and stark naked. But it had to be done. He needed to know. So he asked her, "Which brother are you interested in?"

Whatever she was expecting him to ask, it wasn't this.

Rachel blinked. "What?"

Was she deliberately making this even harder than it already was for him? "It's a simple enough question," he told Rachel, his voice devoid of any emotion. "Which Mendoza brother are you interested in?"

Half a dozen answers sprang to her lips, jockeying for first place. But they all faded back. Rising out of her hurt feelings, none of her possible responses were honest. And she had learned to treasure honesty above all else—even though, right now, she was sorely tempted to shout *Neither of them!*

"I should just throw you out on your ear," she told him. "But if you must have an answer, I'll give you one. It's you. It's been you all along, and I really should have my head examined, because the first man I lose my heart to in five years turns out to be a crazy person." Her hand was back on the doorknob, and she was all set to close the door. All she needed him to do was to take a step back. "All right, you have your answer. Now go."

It had taken a moment for her initial words to sink in.

Him.

She'd picked him.

And that changed everything.

Instantly.

"I have feelings for you, too," he told her quietly, the edge gone from his voice.

As if she really believed that, Rachel thought angrily. "They tell me that's not fatal," she said sarcastically. "You'll get over it."

Suddenly he realized all he stood to lose right at this moment, because he had acted like an idiot. He knew he had to make her understand why he'd come here tonight—and why he'd acted so bullheaded this afternoon.

"I'm serious, Rachel. I don't *want* to get over it. I know I behaved a little strangely today—"

She laughed shortly, interrupting him. "I see you're given to understatement. I had no idea," she told him tersely.

Matteo didn't have a single clue how to start making amends for his behavior or pleading his case, other than to apologize sincerely—as many times as he needed to until the apology finally took.

"Rachel, I'm sorry. I really am," he told her. "It's just that Cisco was acting as if you and he had something going on between you—and I just lost it."

"If that's what you thought, you could have come out and asked me instead of skulking around like some angry, jealous admirer," she told him.

She was right, and he didn't have a leg to stand on if he wanted to mount an argument for his side. His best recourse was to throw himself at her mercy.

"I know," he agreed. "And I behaved like a jackass today."

It was hard to remain angry at a man who was beating himself up for his behavior far better than she could have done.

"Keep going. You're on the right track," Rachel told him.

Matteo instantly noticed that the edge was gone from her voice. It gave him hope that maybe, just maybe, he hadn't completely blown his chances with her. And then, a moment later, Rachel stepped back, opening her door wider, her invitation clear.

"Do you want to come in or keep apologizing until a crowd gathers?" she asked, keeping a completely straight face.

"If that's what it takes to get you to forgive me, then I'll do it."

She was a sucker for sincerity, and he *did* sound sincere.

"You're in luck," she told him. "I'm feeling generous today. I'll take an IOU, though, to be tendered at my discretion."

He could have sworn she sounded serious. Even if she was, he figured maybe he owed it to her.

"You got it." Once inside with the door closed behind him, he took her hands in his, his eyes holding hers. The look in his was repentant and contrite. "I'm really, really sorry, Rachel. It's just that, all my life, Cisco has made a game out of going after anything that mattered to me. He's always liked showing me up and beating me, no matter what the stakes or the prize."

Apart from her father's actions, she always tried to find the positive side of everything. This was no different. "Maybe Cisco's just trying to get you to rise to the challenge, be the best you can be."

He hadn't attributed that sort of noble sentiment to Cisco. His brother had always seemed to be about nothing more serious than having a good time.

However, maybe there was something to what Rachel was saying. But now wasn't the time to delve into the matter. Now was the time to make amends.

"I think you're giving him too much credit," he told her quietly. "In any case, I shouldn't have acted the way I did toward you." Matteo paused, weighing his words carefully. He wanted her to know what had motivated him to behave so badly. "But you have to understand, I thought that he was making a play for you."

"And if he was?" she asked, her tone telling him that it didn't matter what his brother had attempted. He wouldn't have been successful in his endeavor.

"All my life, I've watched women flock to Cisco. All he ever had to do was show up, and if he wanted a girlfriend for the night or the month, he just had to put out his elbow. There'd be a girl hanging off it in no time flat."

"What does that have to do with me?" Rachel wanted to know. "It sounds like you're describing some empty-headed, vapid Valley girl type, not a real, red-blooded American woman." And by that, she made it clear that she meant herself.

Matteo regretted his behavior. "You're right. I should have had more faith in you. It's just that there are times Cisco makes me so angry, I can't see straight."

"But you have so much to offer. Why does what Cisco does—or doesn't do—bother you so much?" she asked. Since he looked so unconvinced, she began to enumerate his good qualities. "You're trustworthy, helpful—"

"Kind, don't forget kind," he interjected. "That's part of the Boy Scout Law, too."

Was he insulted to have those qualities attached to him? "There's nothing wrong with being a Boy Scout," she told him.

She was kidding, right? "Most women aren't attracted to Boy Scouts."

"That depends on who the Boy Scout is," she countered in all seriousness.

Okay, he'd bite, Matteo thought. "And if it's me?" he asked.

"I can foresee tons of women being attracted to those qualities—and to you," she told him, then repeated, "Tons," in a lower, far sexier voice.

That was when Matteo finally gave in to what was going on inside him. Gave in to the passions that were making such urgent demands on him.

Framing Rachel's face with his hands, he leaned in to kiss her.

For just a moment, his heart stopped pounding.

It was supposed to be only a simple make-up kiss, full of contrition, apology and a great deal of relief. Matteo should have known that those three ingredients created a far more volatile reaction when they were combined.

It was as if he'd just had an infusion of molten lava into his veins, shooting all through him, igniting every part of him, especially his desire.

His heart slammed against his chest and then began to pound.

Hard.

He'd thought he had it all under control, but he underestimated the power of his passions when combined with hers. Suddenly, nothing else meant anything. Not time, nor place, nor all those rules he'd always held rigidly in force. The rules all broke apart.

Matteo told himself he was still in control. That he would just allow this momentary aberration to continue for a few more glorious seconds, and then he'd put a stop to it. As painful as it might be to him, he'd pull back. After all, he'd done it before.

But, he quickly discovered, that was then and this

was now. It seemed as if a whole incredibly long life-time had occurred in between.

In place of common sense and control, there was an insatiable insanity that was running riot through him, eagerly savoring every nuance of every kiss, every caress he delivered, every wondrous, silky inch of her that he touched.

Rachel wasn't sure just how it happened. Maybe it had to do with the complete reversal she experienced, going from the depths of an inky sadness to the utter dizzying heights of supreme joy.

Truthfully, she didn't know, couldn't even begin to reasonably speculate. All she knew was that there was this wild squadron of feelings, comprised of peaks and valleys that approximated the giddiness of riding a roller coaster going at top speed.

The only thing she could do was give herself permission to enjoy the sensations as they swept over her one by one while she held on by her fingertips.

Rachel and the man she had lost her heart to went from standing at her door to her sofa. There they assumed various positions while in the throes of the all-consuming passion that had seized them in its viselike grip.

From there they went onto other surfaces—the sofa, the floor—only half-conscious of doing so. Making the halting trip surrounded by a frenzy of heat as they tugged off each other's clothing, desperate for the sensation of bare skin against bare skin.

And all the while, Matteo's strong, full lips were branding her, bringing the ache that was within her up to a full, near-deafening crescendo.

She'd had no idea that a touch so gentle could still

be so provocative, so possessive. Though she kept it to herself, there was no question in her mind that at this very moment, on this page of history, Matteo *owned*—her. She was his from the moment his fingers skimmed along her flesh, no question, no doubt about it.

Rachel kept on kissing him, feeling as if she was never going to get enough of Matteo, never tire of trailing her lips along his skin. And when he returned the favor, she was certain that she was slowly becoming delirious.

She embraced the state, as long as he was there with her.

She was sunshine in a bottle—without the bottle, Matteo thought, unable to believe that what he was experiencing was real. That joy this pure actually existed.

He had never known lovemaking could be like this, had never known that he could *feel* like this. Because he seriously felt as if he could fly and touch the sky— but only as long as she was with him.

If he'd believed in magic, she, here like this with him, would have been the perfect example of it.

The exquisite tension was building up within his body, and he was aware that he couldn't hold back any longer. What it quickly came down to was that it was now—or never.

He chose now.

Matteo pressed her lightly back onto the sofa, then came to her, eager with still a drop of restraint left to him.

His gaze taking hers prisoner, Matteo whispered her name as if he were saying a prayer.

And then he made them one.

The subsequent rhythm that took hold of him captured her as well, and they rode the wave, dancing the eternal dance until they found their way to the very top of the summit.

The gratifying explosion quickly occurred. Fireworks covered them like a sparkling blanket with more than a small amount of euphoria in its weave.

He held on to the feeling for as long as was humanly possible.

Held on to her.

But eventually, the sensation faded back into the shadows, leaving them on the sofa, their bodies and souls entwined, their energy spent.

When he finally found his voice, Matteo quietly said, "I'm sorry."

Her eyes were shut, and she was in a half-dreamlike state. At the sound of his apology, her eyes flew open. She stared at him incredulously. Hurt formed just under her skin.

"For?" she asked, her voice hoarse as she prayed he could find a way out, a way not to shatter this feeling of happiness that was so new to her.

"For earlier. For this afternoon when I first opened the door." And then he summarized it and wrapped it all up with a big baby-blue bow. "For acting like an absolute jerk."

Rachel was extremely relieved. For a moment there, she had thought Matteo was apologizing for making love with her. For her part, she didn't think her heart could have taken that, his apologizing for making love with her.

"You're forgiven," she told him. And then she smiled. "I'd say that, on the whole, everything turned out pretty well, wouldn't you?" she asked teasingly.

"More than well," he agreed, nodding. "I'd even venture to use the word *excellent*."

Rachel considered the word. "Yes, it was," she agreed, then sighed contentedly. "It was excellent."

Matteo propped himself up on one elbow, looking down into her face. He enjoyed the view.

"If I wasn't as exhausted as I am, I'd be tempted to see if I could up the ante," he told her.

"Up the ante?" she repeated, not quite sure what he meant by the gambling term. "How would you go about doing that?"

"You know, see if I can beat my own personal best."

"Where I come from, we don't mess with a perfect thing," she warned him teasingly.

"Are you trying to tell me that I can't mess with you, then?" Matteo asked. There was a twinkle in his eye as he regarded her.

"I wouldn't dream of telling you that," she said, just as she turned her body into his.

"Oh, good," he said, brushing his lips along her shoulder ever so slowly. "Because, as it happens, I'm already dressed for the experience."

She laughed then, and the sound felt good as it echoed through her.

She felt good.

Rachel wasn't sure what the future held, but she

prayed that Matteo Mendoza was in hers and that she was in his.

That, she thought, would make for a totally perfect world in her estimation.

All she could do was hope.

Chapter Eleven

It took Rachel several moments to orient herself as she slowly emerged into a wakeful state. She didn't open her eyes immediately.

The events of the night before seemed to come racing back to her the second she was fully conscious, bringing a rosy glow along with them that filtered all through her. It had been a wondrous night, full of revelations, both about herself and the man she had been so strongly attracted to.

She wanted to wrap her arms around the sensation and hug it to her.

Wanted to hug Matteo.

Rachel turned toward him.

He wasn't there.

Sitting up in her bed, where last night's revelry had eventually brought them, Rachel pulled her knees up to her chest, hugging them instead. She just wanted to allow herself to savor the sensations that were sweeping through her like the tail end of a hurricane.

For the life of her, she'd had no idea that she could react as strongly as she had, nor feel this wild abandonment that had taken possession of her last night. She had been a completely different person with Matteo.

Slowly her smile began to fade as reality, dragging jagged-edged uncertainty behind it, began to wedge its way sharply into her consciousness.

Yes, last night had been wonderful in her estimation, but if it had been wonderful for him as well, why wasn't Matteo still here?

The place beside her where he had lain was cold to her touch. That meant that he had gotten up a while ago.

There were a lot of reasons for him to have left. She got that. And she would have even been fine with that if he had just told her he was going.

If he had just said goodbye.

But he hadn't.

And she couldn't think of a single reason for Matteo to go without either first waking her up or, barring that, leaving her some sort of a note, saying he had to leave. She didn't think she was being too unreasonable, asking for that. She didn't need pages of effusive writing. A couple of lines on a Post-it saying he had to go but he'd call her at the first opportunity he got would have been enough.

It certainly would have made her happy instead of fostering this empty feeling that was beginning to take hold of her very soul.

Suddenly entertaining a shred of hope, Rachel pulled back the covers and lifted Matteo's pillow, hoping that perhaps the note he'd written had gotten lost in the bedding. But it hadn't.

Getting up, she checked under the bed. She found the left sandal she'd lost almost a month ago and a pen she'd been looking for, but no note.

Neither was there one to be found on her bureau.

Or anywhere else in the room.

"Face it, Rach," she murmured under her breath to herself. "He didn't leave you any note."

And any hope that Matteo might still be on the premises, maybe making coffee or even breakfast for the two of them, was quickly yanked away from her when she stopped to listen for the sound of distant movement. A cabinet being closed, a chair scraping along the kitchen floor, *anything*.

There was nothing.

No telltale sounds, no noises to indicate that she wasn't alone in the apartment.

Because she was very much alone.

With a sigh, Rachel sat back down on the bed, feeling dejected, trying very hard to reconcile this disappearing act with the man she'd been with last night. The man who'd disappeared and the man she'd been with last night weren't even close to the same person.

Last night, Matteo had been kind, sensitive, passionate, loving and just about sweetest man who had ever walked the earth. He had been far more than anything she could have hoped for in a lover.

Today, with his disappearing act, he was none of those things.

Maybe he never had been any of those other things,

Rachel suddenly thought. Maybe it had *all* been just an act for him, a means to an end. Maybe what she had actually been for him was a feather in his cap, a trophy he could brag about because he had slept with the woman his brother had indicated that *he* wanted. And Matteo had slept with her when Cisco had not.

That was it, wasn't it? Rachel asked herself, feeling angry tears stinging the inside corners of her eyes. She was the prize at the end of the tug-of-war Matteo's father had told her that Matteo was forever waging with Cisco.

That had to be it.

Why else would he just disappear without a trace like this the morning after they'd made love? The only thing that made sense was that he felt he'd gotten what he came for. Once he had, he left. It was as simple as that.

And that made *her* a prize-winning fool, Rachel thought, feeling both ashamed and madder than hell.

What was *wrong* with her? she silently demanded as she went into her bathroom to take a quick shower. She was supposed to be smart enough not to be utterly blinded like that by someone like Matteo.

Good looks only went so far. Integrity and dedication were the real turn-on in her life, and apparently Matteo Mendoza had neither integrity nor any sort of loyalty to speak of. When she'd been at the top of her game, she would have seen through Matteo in a heartbeat. Instead, her heartbeat wound up blinding her to his flaws.

And now it was obviously time to pay for it, she thought bitterly.

Squaring her shoulders as she stepped into the

shower, Rachel attempted to give herself a pep talk. After all, she had already endured a great deal in her short life, uprooting herself and leaving everyone she knew—or *thought* she knew—behind. This was just another bump along the way.

"This, too, shall pass," she murmured under her breath, trying to think herself past the hurt she was feeling, even as the water from the shower head mingled with the tears that wouldn't stop flowing.

Although Matteo hated to admit it—even if it was only to himself—fear had made him leave Rachel's bed in the middle of the night.

Fear of what he might see in her eyes when she looked at him in the morning.

If he saw regret there—or even just a glimmer of regret—it would tear him apart. Better not to have been with Rachel at all than to see the regret that the deed had created and brought forth there in her eyes.

Doubts and uncertainty about what had transpired between them had crept in the moment the last of the breathtaking euphoria had finally receded, slipping away from him.

They had made love twice last night, and as impossible as it seemed, the second time had been even better than the first. The second time, he'd known what to expect, yet somehow it had still wound up being a joyous surprise because of the intensity that had woven itself in and through the familiarity that was there beneath the top layer.

But as with all good things, eventually that had faded into the shadows, leaving darkness in its place. Darkness and the specter of mind-numbing disappointment, the silent passenger who had ridden in during the night, ready to undermine every single thing that had happened the moment morning's first light seeped into Rachel's small, cozy bedroom.

Matteo knew only one thing for certain. That he had never felt like this before—fearful—because he'd never experienced this sort of a surging high before, one that grasped hold of him and just made everything a hundredfold better.

Lovemaking, when it occurred in his life, had always been, for the most part, an enjoyable activity. But it never bore any consequences, and the pleasure it brought would disappear into the past for him practically the moment it happened. Certainly within a few hours.

But from the first moment he had taken Rachel into his arms, he knew that this was going to be different.

And it was.

Because *she* mattered.

He'd thought he'd lost her before anything ever began because Cisco seemed so interested in her and because his brother had deliberately asked her out, moving quickly right in front of him. It was as if Cisco was rubbing Matteo's nose in the fact that if he wanted someone, all he had to do was snap his fingers and she was his.

Had Cisco asked her out like that because he was as taken with Rachel as he was? Or was it because Cisco saw how taken *he* was with Rachel and that was enough of a reason for his brother to try to steal her away?

He had no answer for that.

It was all so complicated.

Making love with Rachel should have settled things for him. Instead, it just confused them even further. Matteo felt perplexed, vulnerable and at a total loss as to his next step—if one was to even be taken.

He would have felt better about his course of action if he'd known for certain that Rachel would remain with him, that last night had not been a onetime thing but the beginning of a long relationship.

Matteo knew that he was in it for the long haul, but what if she wasn't? What if she had made love with him last night to get back at Cisco for taking her for granted?

Or maybe she made love with him because she felt sorry for him. That would have hurt worst of all, he thought.

All these thoughts and self-doubts had been assaulting him as he slipped out of her bed and gathered up his scattered clothing from the floor. Carrying them into the living room, Matteo quickly hurried into his jeans and shirt.

Then, carrying his shoes, he tiptoed out of the apartment and pulled the door closed behind him.

The click of the lock told him that he had taken an irreversible step. Even if he changed his mind about this and wanted to slip back into her bed, he couldn't.

The matter had been settled for him.

He had to move on.

Rachel desperately wanted to call Matteo, to yell at him; to ask him calmly why he had left her apartment so abruptly, without a note or anything; to tell him that she never wanted to see him again.

A hundred different conversations materialized in

her head, each one with a different approach, each eventually being shot down.

The only thing they had in common with each other was that the hundred different conversations all included the word *why?* in them.

She desperately wanted to know why.

By the time she had gotten ready and was driving to work, Rachel had managed to semi-convince herself that what had happened was really for the best. Not the night of lovemaking, but specifically her waking up to find him gone.

If, as she was now beginning to suspect, Matteo had just been there to get what he could from her and, once that was accomplished, he was just intent on moving on, then at least she was spared the agonizing decision she might have been faced with down the line. Namely, having to tell Matteo about her father. If they had remained together, she would have to explain her past to him, a past she was trying to divorce herself from.

She would have to tell him that she had left home because she had discovered her father had been living a lie, a lie he'd had his whole family believing in since the day she had been born. A lie he had perpetuated for her entire life.

Most likely the entire lives of all her siblings. None of them had ever acted as if they had discovered this massive cover-up her father had engineered to erase his tracks.

"This massive *lie*. Call a spade a spade, Rach," she lectured herself.

She felt that her father's secret shouldn't continue to be covered up any longer, but she didn't want to hurt her siblings or her mother. Every day that went by without his confession was another day he spent living a lie.

All those late nights her father had claimed to be at the office, working—they had been late nights, all right, but late nights spent perpetuating the legend of his life and indulging his appetites.

She was willing to bet on it.

It wasn't something she intended to make public, but in all honesty, eventually she would have to tell the person she was seriously involved with about this.

For now, of course, that was nobody, Rachel thought. Her heart felt heavy over the admission, especially when she tried to excise the very image of Matteo from her mind.

So far, that was *not* working.

She was relieved that at least for today, her workday began and ended in The Hollows Cantina. She sincerely doubted she would see any of the Mendoza men here. After all, Orlando lived in Horseback Hollow, so it was only to be expected that he would eat most of his meals at home. And now that his two sons were visiting him here, all three would undoubtedly eat at his house.

She was safe, Rachel told herself. She repeated that to herself probably a dozen times in the space of a few hours.

Even so, every time the front door opened, her heart would leap up to her throat and then take a while to settle down into place again.

At this rate, Rachel was fairly convinced that she was going to be a wreck by the dinner shift, if not before.

"So how is it going?"

The question, catching her off guard, came from Wendy Fortune Mendoza, who circled around until she faced her. Wendy, along with her husband, Marcos, owned the Cantina. It was their first real business venture together, opened after their changes to the Mendoza family's first restaurant in Red Rock, Red, proved to be such a huge success.

Wendy was checking on the Cantina's operations to make sure everything was running smoothly and no adjustments needed to be made. The Cantina was her and Marcos's baby, and as it had only been open for a few months, it was still in its infancy. She wanted to do whatever it took to make this restaurant a success.

Rachel looked at the woman, startled by her question. It sounded harmless on the surface, but was it? Wendy was a Fortune by birth. Did she suspect Rachel's secret? Was that the reason for her question?

Or was she asking about Matteo, about how it was going between them?

That seemed the more likely question. Wendy was probably asking because of her husband, who was also a Mendoza.

Rachel tried to be as vague as possible about what was—or wasn't—happening between her and Matteo without being rude.

"I really don't know," she told Wendy. "All right, I guess. It's too soon to tell. I don't know if there's going to be another one," she said, referring to a date, since that was what she assumed Wendy was asking about.

Wendy looked at her. "Another one? I doubt it. At least, not so soon."

She was right. Rachel's heart sank. "Then he's talked to you?"

"No, but he doesn't have to," Wendy replied. "Some things you just know. Maybe in a year or so, but not now."

"A year?" Rachel echoed, now thoroughly confused. "He expects me to wait a year?" Talk about being overly confident—

"Wait, what?" Wendy cried, staring at Rachel. "Who expects you to wait a year?"

"Matteo," Rachel said, more confused than ever. "Aren't we talking about your husband's cousin?"

"I thought we were talking about my husband's decisions about the restaurant." Wendy began to laugh at the obvious error that almost seemed to have a life of its own for a few go-rounds. "Perhaps we should start from the beginning," she suggested once she stopped laughing.

Rachel blew out a breath. A wave of unexpected relief washed over her. She really hadn't wanted to discuss—or even think about—Matteo right now. She smiled at Wendy. "Perhaps we should."

Chapter Twelve

Wendy tried again, this time being more articulate and specific in her questioning.

"What I was trying to ask you was how you think things are going *here* at the Cantina. In other words, do the customers appear to be satisfied? Do you think there's something that can be improved upon, or brought in, or eliminated from the menu that would make dining here a much more pleasurable experience for the customers?" Wendy paused for half a second, allowing her question to sink in before continuing, "I also want to know if you have any personal complaints about the working conditions here."

"Personal complaints?" Rachel echoed. While she could understand why the woman was interested in keeping the customer happy, she was more than a little surprised by Wendy's second question regarding her feelings about the state of the working conditions.

"Yes. Personal complaints," Wendy repeated with emphasis. "Do you find the work atmosphere here too stressful, too difficult to put up with on a regular basis?" She became even more specific by asking, "Is the assistant manager too demanding?"

"Julia?" Rachel asked incredulously.

Julia Tierney, the former grocery store manager, had lobbied strongly for Marcos and Wendy Mendoza to select Horseback Hollow as the site for their second restaurant. Her hard work had eventually paid off, changing many people's minds as well as making the case for this location to Marcos and Wendy. Julia was at least *half* the reason that the restaurant was built in Horseback Hollow and not somewhere else.

To show both their gratitude and their loyalty to someone who had been so instrumental in helping them, the couple had installed the former grocery store manager as their assistant manager at the Cantina.

Julia loved running the restaurant. Everyone who worked for her knew that.

"What can I say?" Rachel asked. "Julia's a great boss. If one of the girls calls in sick, Julia pitches in and takes her place. I've never seen her try to lord it over anyone. And no, I definitely have no personal complaints.

"As to your first question," Rachel continued, "from everything I can see, the customers seem very happy with the service and the actual meals themselves."

When the Cantina had opened up in June last

year, it had been regarded by some as too upscale for
their taste—a real "rich folks" restaurant—but after
a while, the detractors had come around. The atmosphere here was warm and friendly.

"I'd say that the customers think the food was excellent, the prices reasonable and the service—" here
she grinned broadly, lumping herself in with the rest
of the group "—exceedingly friendly and outgoing."

Rachel knew that there were still going to be those
few who would complain, but those were just hard-
ened malcontents who were never really happy unless
they could find fault with something. As far as she
was concerned, those people were to be disregarded.

"Thank you for being so honest with me and letting me pick your brain for a minute," Wendy told her.
The next moment, the co-owner drew a little closer
to her so that she wouldn't be accidentally overheard
by any of the other servers. In a lower tone of voice,
Wendy asked her, "Now, would you like to tell me
what the problem is with Matteo?"

The moment the man's name was mentioned, Rachel's nerves began jumping and doing somersaults
inside her.

"Problem?" Rachel repeated, trying her best to
look puzzled. "What makes you think there's a problem?"

Wendy's eyes met hers, as if to say *Oh, puh-leazze*.
But she allowed the young woman her dignity and
addressed the question seriously. "Because he was
the first thing you thought of when I asked you how
it was going. Has he done something to upset you?"

Rachel pressed her lips together, uncomfortable

with the topic. "I'd really rather not talk about it, Mrs. Mendoza."

"No need to be so formal, Rachel," Wendy told her. "You can call me Wendy. And as for the rest of it, I understand totally." She leaned her head a little closer before saying, "The Mendoza men can be utterly infuriating, and the worst part of it is that they don't even realize it.

"But they are worth the trouble if you have the patience to wait them out until they finally come around. I vividly remember what it was like, being your age and unsure of almost every move I made. Not only that, but my own family regarded me as a black sheep, never managing to see things through, bringing them only heartache and grief. It took a lot for me to turn things around. I just want you to know that nothing is beyond your reach if you want it badly enough." Wendy closed the topic for now, adding only, "I am available if you find you need to vent." With that, Wendy patted the hostess on her shoulder just before she began to walk away.

And then she abruptly stopped. Swinging back around to look at Rachel, she announced, "Incoming. Ten o'clock sharp."

For a second, Rachel had no idea what the Cantina's co-owner was saying to her. And then she realized Wendy was alerting her to the fact that someone was coming in, pushing open the front door.

Not just someone but *that* someone.

Matteo.

Rachel instantly stiffened.

Wendy's protective, mothering instincts rose to the

surface instantly. "Want me to stick around, be your wing lady?" she offered Rachel.

Rachel shook her head. "No, I'm fine, but thank you for offering."

She had left the old Rachel behind five years ago, when she'd left home and forced herself to become independent of her family *and* their money. She was not about to hide behind anyone for any reason, especially not because she was facing an uncomfortable situation. Dealing with that sort of thing was all just part of being an adult, and Rachel was determined not to slide backward.

Matteo hadn't wanted to come here this morning. But he knew that the longer he put this off, the harder it was going to be and the larger the specter of what was between Rachel and him would grow.

He needed to have this one-on-one with Rachel before his nerves became too great to handle.

Walking in, Matteo looked around the Cantina to see if he could spot her.

"Table for one?" the hostess at the front desk asked him cheerfully.

"Two," the deep male voice coming from behind him corrected the hostess. "Table for two."

Managing to hide the fact that he had been caught by surprise, Matteo swung around to look accusingly at his brother.

"What are you doing here?" he demanded. Cisco hadn't been there a minute ago. Nor had he seen his brother's car when he'd parked his own close to the restaurant a couple of minutes ago.

Cisco's grin was wide and charming—at least to

everyone but Matteo. "I thought you might like some company."

Matteo narrowed his eyes. "You thought wrong." He didn't want to cause a scene, but neither did he want his brother here with him. He couldn't say what he had come to say if Cisco was anywhere within hearing range.

"Nobody comes to a restaurant to be alone, little brother," Cisco told him. "That's what drive-throughs are for. Tell you what," Cisco proposed magnanimously, "my treat."

Matteo had no intentions of accepting his brother's money or being bought off with a plate of enchiladas. "I don't need you paying for me," Matteo retorted.

Cisco changed directions faster than a sidewinder making his way across the sand. "Okay, your treat. I promise not to order the most expensive thing on the menu."

While Matteo was trying to rid himself of his brother, the woman at the reception desk had beckoned over the closest waitress.

"I'll do that," Rachel told the waitress. She wasn't officially on duty yet and she wanted an excuse to see just what was going on between the brothers.

"Sure," the waitress said, stepping back.

Taking in a breath, Rachel made her way over to the reception desk. She picked up two menus along her route.

"Ah, we meet again," Cisco declared, his broad grin never wavering. "It must be fate, don't you think so, Matteo?" he asked glibly, turning toward his brother. When the latter made no reply, Cisco looked from him to the young woman, who then turned on her heel and began to lead them to their table. Stony silence accompanied them.

"Is it just me," Cisco asked, "or has the temperature suddenly drastically dropped? It's like there's an artic breeze blowing through here," he noted, still being annoyingly cheerful.

"It's you," Matteo bit off between clenched teeth.

This was like a nightmare. He'd come here to try to explain himself to Rachel as best he could. He didn't really expect her to believe him, but he wanted her to know that his leaving her bed before she was awake had nothing to do with her—at least not the way she probably thought it did.

But he couldn't say any of that if Cisco was right there, listening to every word he uttered.

Turning to Cisco as Rachel brought them to their table, he told his older brother, "I want you to get lost."

"Can't," Cisco replied glibly. "I know my way around too well."

Matteo should have known that there would be no cooperation coming from Cisco. "Then go somewhere else," he said.

Cisco made himself comfortable, sitting down first. "But this is the best restaurant in town, Mattie," he teased, "and I'm hungry."

Matteo had a solution for that. He struggled to hold on to his temper. He couldn't have a meltdown in public. That would make him look unstable in Rachel's eyes—and that was the *last* thing he wanted.

Looking at Rachel, he told her, "Whatever he orders—" he jerked a thumb in his brother's direction "—make it to go."

Cisco laughed drily. "Boy, you certainly don't make a brother feel welcome."

"There's a reason for that—you're not," Matteo told him point-blank.

Yes, at bottom they were brothers, and if called upon, Matteo would come to Cisco's aid and do a great deal for his brother, but right now all he wanted was to have his brother get up and go away.

"Lucky for you I'm not thin-skinned," Cisco informed him.

"Right, lucky. Order," Matteo instructed him, pointing at the lunch selections.

Cisco ordered, but he took his time about it, reading every description of every one of the different lunch entrees and specials the Cantina offered out loud. Only then did he make his choice: beef and bean enchiladas as well as a tostada salad.

"Is that your lunch," Matteo asked Cisco, "or the meal you intend to consume before you go into hibernation?"

"Just lunch," Cisco replied brightly. "I'm hungry— especially since my little brother's paying for it."

It was getting more and more difficult to hold on to his temper, Matteo thought. "What did I say about calling me that?"

Cisco's eyes crinkled as he grinned in amusement. It really was too easy, he thought, getting his brother's dander up. "Are you going to beat me up right here, in front of witnesses?"

Their eyes met and held for a long moment. Matteo did his best to get himself under control, refusing to allow Cisco to win the round. "Why do you do it?" Matteo wanted to know.

"Do what?" Cisco asked as if he really had no idea what his brother was talking about.

Matteo chose his words carefully, determined not to make himself look like a hothead—or an idiot. "Tear me down all the time."

Cisco regarded him in silence for a moment, then said something that Matteo hadn't been prepared for. "To get you to build yourself back up again. Every time you do, you're a little bit stronger, a little bit feistier, a little bit more confident than the version that came just before."

"You're crazy," Matteo accused him.

Cisco had just made that up on the spur of the moment, Matteo thought. His brother was a playboy. He always had been. To him, it had always been about winning the girl of the moment, the one he set his sights on. If Cisco thought Matteo was interested in her as well, all the better because the stakes went up. There was nothing noble about it.

"Like a fox," Cisco countered.

It never ceased to amaze Matteo how his brother always manipulated things to make himself come out on top. "That's not how I see it."

"And you're entitled to your opinion," Cisco said. "Doesn't make you right, but you're still entitled to your opinion."

And then Cisco easily slipped into his ultra-charming mode as he watched Rachel return to their table. The tray she was carrying had Matteo's order on it as well as Cisco's, which was bundled in a large, sturdy paper bag with the Cantina logo stamped on both sides.

"You have your breakfast," Matteo said the moment Rachel had once again left their table. "Now leave."

Cisco shook his head like a teacher whose lesson had fallen on deaf ears. "You really have to work on your social graces, Mattie."

Matteo looked his brother in the eye. "You have no idea how hard I'm working on them right this minute."

Cisco laughed, appearing genuinely to enjoy this exchange between them. "I get the message. Two's company and all that."

Matteo's eyes darkened. "Get out of here now," he ordered in a barely audible voice.

"Needs a little more work," Cisco pronounced, obviously still pretending to assess the effects of his handiwork on his brother, "but pretty good." With that, he took the supersize doggie bag and rose from the table. "See you around, Matteo."

It seemed rather inevitable that they *would* see each other around at some point, given all the Mendozas in town, but Matteo for one was going to work as hard as he could to keep their paths from crossing with any sort of frequency.

Because his trust for Cisco had eroded to nearly nothing by now, Matteo made a point of watching his brother not just walk away from the table, but leave the restaurant entirely.

Only when his brother was truly good and gone did he turn his attention to the reason he had come here in the first place.

Rachel.

She was all the way across the room, seating another table. He watched patiently, waiting until she finally looked in his direction in an unguarded moment.

The second she did, he raised his hand, calling her over.

Reluctantly, concerned about what he might say now that his brother was gone, she made her way over to Matteo's table.

"Is there something wrong with your meal, sir?" Rachel asked in the most detached, distant voice she could summon.

How did they get here after last night? The question nagged at him. Could there be this amount of animosity because he had left without a word? Apparently the answer to that was yes, he thought as he tried to surface above the guilt.

"No, there's nothing wrong with the meal. It's fine. What's not fine is the problem between us," he told her. "I came here to talk to you."

Rachel glanced over her shoulder to see if either Wendy or Julia was anywhere in the vicinity, watching her. They weren't.

"I'm sorry," she told him crisply. "I can't have any long conversations with the customers while I'm working," she lied. "It's against restaurant policy."

That seemed simple enough to circumvent. "Then go on your break."

As if she could just snap her fingers and have it happen. "I—"

"Please?" he added with such sincerity, it got through all the protective layers of indifference she'd been busy wrapping around herself ever since she'd woken that morning.

Rachel suppressed a deep sigh. She had every right to be angry at this man and just cut him dead every time their paths crossed from here on in.

So why did all her fine resolutions, all the promises that she had made to herself, just dissolve like so many soap bubbles dancing in the wind when he looked at her with those big, brown, contrite eyes of his?

Why couldn't she stand firm instead of melting like a scoop of ice cream that had fallen onto the concrete in the dead of summer?

"Wait here. I'll see what I can do," she told him, her voice strained. With that, she left his table and disappeared behind the rear of the reception desk. She was looking for Julia, who made up their weekly and daily schedules.

Rachel was gone for several minutes.

Long enough for him to think that perhaps she had said whatever she needed to in order to make an exit, and once she had, she had chosen to give him the slip. For all he knew, she might have told her boss that she felt sick and was, even now, on her way home, leaving him here with his food getting cold.

So now what?

Was he just going to sit here until doomsday, waiting for a woman who wasn't about to return? Just how many times did he have to be hit by a two-by-four before he moved out of range?

Taking out his wallet, he removed several bills and was about to leave them on the table to pay for both Cisco's meal and his own when he heard her voice. Rachel was talking to someone close by, a redhead who looked vaguely familiar. He'd probably met her at some family function or other, Matteo thought.

The next moment, he realized that Rachel was getting permission to take her break earlier than scheduled.

And she had done it because he'd asked her to.

It was a promising start, he thought.

Now, as she sat down and joined him, it was up to him to keep the promising start going so that it turned into something that bore fruit.

He crossed his fingers.

Chapter Thirteen

"All right, I don't have that much time," Rachel said.

She folded her hands in front of her on the table like someone who had resigned herself to getting something distasteful but inevitable over with, ideally as quickly as possible.

"You wanted to talk," she told him coldly, "so talk."

He had just the one chance to have this come out right, Matteo thought. One chance to try to make her understand why he had left her bed so abruptly last night. At the same time, he needed to word his reason in a way that wouldn't place him in too negative a light.

Some negativity was inevitable. He knew that. But he also knew that a balance had to be struck. If it wasn't, how could he expect her to consider having a relationship with someone who behaved more like an adolescent than a man?

No matter what was said to the contrary, most women wanted to be with bad boys and heroes. Wishy-washy and indecisive were not part of the description when women went looking for the man they would regard as their other half.

All he could be, Matteo thought, was honest with her and hope for the best.

"Last night," he began, his eyes meeting hers, "was without a doubt the singularly most fantastic night of my life."

Rachel wanted so *badly* to believe him. "If that's true," she said skeptically, "what happened to you? Were you kidnapped by aliens who refused to give you any time to leave a note, some kind of an explanation as to why you suddenly had to dash off into the night?

"Who *does* that kind of thing?" she demanded. "I'll tell you who. Men who don't give a damn about anyone's feelings but their own. Who are only interested in their own satisfaction—and don't care who they hurt as long as they get what they want."

Her eyes were blazing as she spoke, but there was still a tiny glimmer within her, maybe even less than tiny, that hoped he'd come up with something she could believe. Something that would make her want to forgive him.

She didn't want to feel this way about him—but what choice did she have?

"Are you finished?" Matteo asked quietly after a beat had gone by.

"Very," she retorted. She was a fool for thinking he could explain his actions away to her satisfaction, she thought in disgust.

She began to rise from her chair, but Matteo put

his hand on hers, silently pleading with her to remain where she was.

"Would it help to say I was very, very sorry?" he asked.

"No," she responded firmly. But then, because last night had turned her entire world upside down, Rachel willed herself to give him just a little more time to plead his case. "But it's a start," she said more magnanimously. "Go on."

He gave it to her straight. "I've told you I'm not very confident when it comes to women, Rachel. I wish I were, but I'm not. I'm not Cisco," he emphasized.

Why would he think that she wanted him to be more like his brother? "I didn't pick Cisco. I picked *you*," she reminded him.

Maybe he'd just won by default, Matteo thought. "But you did go out with him."

Was he going to hold *that* against her? Seriously? "Only one time, Matteo. Because he asked, and at the time, I had no reason to turn him down."

She had a point, and if the subject wasn't such a sensitive one for him, he would have backed her sentiments all the way.

Still, he needed to have something settled in his own mind before he put all this to rest. "So there's nothing between you and Cisco?" he asked.

Part of Rachel wanted to just get up and walk away without saying a word, making Matteo stew about the situation the way he had made her agonize over finding herself alone this morning, causing a stampede of self-doubt to come storming through her as she tried to figure out what she could possibly have done to cause him to leave like that.

But it was specifically *because* she had gone through all that herself that she couldn't make another human being go through the haunting uncertainty that she'd been dealing with these past few hours. So she *didn't* just get up and walk away.

Revenge was not part of her makeup. It never had been. She was better than that.

"No," she answered Matteo, "not in the way you mean." She saw the question in his eyes. So there would be no further misunderstanding, she elaborated. "Cisco is a charming *acquaintance*. Maybe someday he'll even become a friend, but that's it. Nothing more," she emphasized. With that, she glanced at her watch, as if she was running out of her allotted minutes. "Anything else?"

He had a feeling that he still hadn't managed to make her understand what it was like, living in his brother's shadow.

He tried again. "All my life, I've felt…well, outshined, I guess, by Cisco." The shrug was partially hapless. "I think I might even have unconsciously used that as an excuse." He could see that she still didn't understand, not that he blamed her. He was having trouble coming to terms with this self-analysis himself. "Whenever I didn't get what I had set out to get, I blamed it on him rather than myself for not trying hard enough. It was easier that way, I guess, having a built-in excuse. Saying that Cisco was faster, better, smarter, handsomer." He blew out a breath, forcing himself to continue, "I used that as an excuse to avoid moving forward."

Rachel's eyes never left his. "You know that's not right, don't you?"

"What's not right?" he asked, confused. "Moving forward?"

"No, the part where you said Cisco was smarter, better, handsomer." Someone else might have said those things fishing for a compliment, but not Matteo. That much she knew about him. He was not full of himself in any sense of the word. And he obviously didn't realize his own self-worth. "None of that's true. You're all those things when you want to be."

It was on the tip of his tongue to discount her words, saying something to the effect that she probably felt obligated to compliment him for the sake of being polite.

But there was something about the way Rachel said it, the way she sounded, that made him pause. "You mean that?" he asked.

"I wouldn't say it if I didn't." A small, private smile curved the corners of her mouth and filtered into her eyes as she thought of the way they'd been last night. The way *he'd* been last night. Gentle, caring and then wildly passionate, bringing every fiber of her being to life. "I was there, remember?"

"I remember," he replied in a low voice that was overflowing with emotion. "I remember every single magical moment of it."

Reaching across the small table, Matteo took her hands in his. Looking into her eyes, he did something he wouldn't normally do. He went out on that very shaky limb, leaving himself totally exposed. He knew there might be a chance she would begin to have doubts the moment she walked away—unless he did this. "I need to tell you something."

"Talk quickly," she urged him, looking at her watch again. "My break's almost over."

Matteo shook his head. "This isn't something that I can say quickly." Granted, it was only one sentence, but he needed time to work up to it. What he had to tell her demanded that it have time before as well as after so the words, the sentiment, could be given the respect they both deserved and commanded. "Could I pick you up after your shift?" he asked.

Rachel had driven her car here, and there were logistics to take into consideration, but the bottom line was that he was asking her out, she thought. Asking her out so that he could get this—whatever *this* was— off his chest. She'd already made up her mind to give him another chance.

"Sure," Rachel replied. "I get off at six today."

"Six it is," he told her.

And then she hurried away.

Matteo whistled as he paid his tab and left the restaurant, a smile on his face.

"Judging by your smile," Wendy commented as Rachel passed the co-owner on her way to wait on a new table, "I see that my cousin has managed to redeem himself."

"He's working on it," Rachel replied.

The smile on her lips told her boss that she strongly suspected Matteo would manage to accomplish exactly what he set out to do.

"What's that?" Matteo asked, nodding at the very large paper bag Rachel was carrying when he met her in front of the Cantina six hours later.

"Your cousin's wife insisted I take this for you,"

Rachel told him, keeping a very straight face. "She said she thought you'd be hungry after having nothing but humble pie to eat this morning."

"Humble pie?" he repeated, not quite certain what the other woman had meant. Assuming that it was heavy, he took the bag with its carefully packed collection of small containers from her. He was right. The bag was heavier than it looked.

Rachel nodded. "It's a figure of speech, referring to—"

Matteo held up his hand. "I know what it is," he told her, cutting her explanation short. "What I'm wondering about is how she would even know anything about our situation."

He personally had less than a nodding acquaintance with the pretty brunette his cousin had married. For that matter, he knew only Marcos by sight. He doubted if he and the other man had ever exchanged more than a couple of words at any one time.

Had Rachel been talking to the woman, unloading— and perhaps even complaining—as some women were prone to doing?

"That's easy enough," Rachel told him. "Wendy saw you—and Cisco—at the Cantina this morning, remember?"

Matteo felt contrite. He should have known that Rachel wouldn't do anything to either compromise his integrity or embarrass the hell out of him in any way.

Mentally he apologized to her, silently promising to make amends.

"Now I do," he admitted. "I have to confess that when I'm around you, I have a tendency to forget a lot of other details—like how to breathe," he said, lowering his voice just for a moment.

She was not about to allow herself to get carried away with that imagery. It would be all too easy to do that, and she had to remain grounded, she reminded herself. After all, she wasn't exactly the best judge of character, now, was she? She'd thought the world of her father—and look how wrong she'd been about *that*.

So she made light of what Matteo had just told her. "You could try writing that in a dark, indelible marker on the inside of your wrist. That way you won't ever forget—and accidentally wind up asphyxiating."

He glanced at his wrist, as if momentarily considering her suggestion and envisioning something being written there.

"Indelible marker, huh? I think I'll just take my chances with my memory," Matteo said.

There was amusement in her eyes. "Just trying to help. You said you had something you wanted to talk to me about," she reminded him.

"We can get to it after dinner," he told her, nodding at the bag he had taken from her.

Rachel looked at him knowingly—and somewhat amused, as well. "You know you're just stalling, right?"

Matteo made no attempt to deny it. "Yes, but in the best possible way," he said glibly.

Mentally he crossed his fingers and hoped that she would understand and agree with his assessment once she knew what he wanted to tell her.

Rachel sighed with a touch of drama. "Wendy was right."

Maybe he *should* get to know Wendy better, at least while he was still in Horseback Hollow. She seemed to have considerable influence with Rachel. "Right about what?"

"She said that Mendoza men require a lot of patience." Taking the large bag back, she put it on the floor of the passenger side in her vehicle, then turned toward Matteo. "We'll each drive our own cars. You can follow me."

She told him that just in case he'd forgotten how to get to her apartment. She knew how easily bruised male egos became when asking for directions. Some would rather wander around endlessly than admit they needed help.

"To the ends of the earth," Matteo told her willingly.

"To guest parking at my complex will be good enough," she quipped, grinning as she thought over his words.

"Consider it done," Matteo told her.

His car was parked two rows behind hers. Moving quickly, he hurried over to it now and started it immediately, pumping the accelerator to give it extra gas. The car all but roared in response, ready to tear out of the parking lot like the proverbial bat out of hell.

That made two of them, Matteo thought.

He couldn't stop smiling all the way over to her place.

"Looks like Wendy had the chef pack a little bit of everything that was on tonight's menu," Rachel told Matteo, peeking into the bag once they were inside her apartment. She smiled as she looked up at him.

"I guess she thinks maybe you're in need of some fattening up."

He laughed shortly, helping Rachel unpack the various small containers and placing them on her kitchen counter for the time being.

"That makes it sound like I'm a Thanksgiving turkey that needs to gain some weight in order to make an acceptable meal."

"Not to worry," she told him, patting his face before moving to open the cupboard. "Nobody's going to be pulling on your drumstick."

"Well, there go all my plans for the evening," Matteo said, snapping his fingers.

"Those were all your plans?" she asked, amusement tugging at the corners of her mouth.

He looked at her significantly. He could feel his temperature rising just looking at her. "Well, most of them, at any rate," he joked.

They were both skirting around the real reason for his being here. She grew serious. "So what was it that you had to tell me?"

"Eating first, remember?" Matteo reminded her, taking down some of her dishes so they could empty the different containers and place them all on her table for a sit-down meal.

"Boy, you certainly know how to draw something out, don't you?" Rachel marveled, although she made no effort to get him to say whatever it was he wanted to tell her now. If it turned out to be something she didn't want to hear, she could definitely wait to have it out in the open.

"Think of it as a cliff-hanger," Matteo suggested, getting out her utensils. "Except people aren't hanging onto a ledge by their fingertips," he said when she looked at him quizzically. "It's more of an emotional cliffhanger."

"If you say so," Rachel murmured. Looking around, she checked to make sure she hadn't forgotten to put out anything Wendy had sent home with her.

Now who's stalling? she silently asked herself.

Satisfied that everything was out, she gestured for Matteo to take a seat. "Everything looks so good," she observed, still standing next to the table, "I honestly don't know where to start."

"I do," he told her.

"Where?" she asked, curious as to what out of the entire spread appealed to him most. She turned to look at him.

That was when he kissed her, softly brushing his lips against hers, sending her heart racing wildly.

"Does that answer your question?" he asked in a low tone.

His words seemed to dance along her skin.

Rachel didn't say a word, didn't trust her voice not to crack. Instead, she just nodded her head, her hastily gathered-up ponytail swishing to and fro to some inner rhythmic tune that only she was privy to.

When she could finally speak again, she uttered only a single word: "Yes." It was another couple of minutes before she could give voice to what she was thinking. "But when we finish eating dinner, you have to tell me what it is you wanted to tell me back in the restaurant. Do we have a deal?" she asked, putting out her hand to Matteo.

He enveloped it in his and shook it. "We have a deal," he agreed.

* * *

It seemed to Rachel that he was taking an inordinate amount of time finishing his meal.

Maybe it was her imagination, but Matteo seemed to be chewing far slower than a man of his age and energy should be able to.

"It's because of what you have to tell me, isn't it?" she finally asked. All through the meal, she'd ignored the elephant in the room, but now it was time to do something with the animal.

"What is?" he asked innocently.

"The way you're eating your dinner," she said, gesturing at his plate. "You're practically chewing in slow motion."

"Chewing too quickly results in people choking on their food." He was teasing her now—and maybe stalling just a little. If she took what he had to say badly, then it was all over. This was for all the marbles—or nothing at all.

"No chance of that happening," she assured him. And then, after giving the matter another few moments, she told him, "It's okay."

Now he actually *was* confused. "What is?"

"You don't have to tell me what you wanted to say earlier today."

He opened his mouth to speak, but she held her hand up, wanting him to hear her out completely before making up his mind or saying anything.

"If you've decided that you'd rather keep whatever it was to yourself, that's okay. I understand. I wouldn't want you to—"

"I love you."

Chapter Fourteen

Her eyes widened as she stared at Matteo across the table in utter disbelief. She was positive that she had imagined the whole thing, or at the very least, misheard him. Both sounded far more plausible to her than the words she'd heard coming from him.

Still, she had to ask, had to be sure. "What did you say?"

Matteo enunciated each word clearly as he repeated, "I love you."

The three words shimmered in the air between them like carefully cut prisms in the morning sun. Matteo held his breath, watching her face, waiting to see her reaction.

Praying.

He had just risked absolutely everything. Had he made a complete fool of himself—or had he just won the biggest prize of his life?

Stunned, for a moment, Rachel couldn't think, couldn't speak. And then, afraid to allow herself to be swept up in what could turn out to be an impossible fantasy, she protested, "How can you love me? You don't even know me."

They had a difference of opinion on that, Matteo thought. "I know all I need to know."

"No, you don't," she told him in a voice so quiet it unsettled him.

"All right," he said, bracing himself. "Then tell me." He sincerely doubted that *anything* she had to say would change how he felt about her.

But she shook her head. Her father was still a very raw spot for her. Maybe someday it wouldn't be, but that day wasn't now.

"I don't want to talk about it."

Rachel was really making this difficult, he thought. Once or twice during their conversations within the past week or so, he'd gotten the feeling that she was hiding something. But given the woman he had come to know, he'd decided to shrug it off. After all, just how bad could it be?

However, the look on her face now gave him pause. He might as well get a couple of things cleared up and out of the way.

"Did you kill someone?" he asked Rachel out of the blue.

The question caught her completely off guard. "No, of course not."

"Then it can't be that bad," he concluded. The look in her eyes told him he was wrong in his assessment. He took into account who he was dealing with. Rachel had a tendency to magnify her own flaws. "Look, we've all done things we're not proud of, things we wouldn't exactly want to become public knowledge.

"But the important thing is that we get beyond it. That we learn from whatever we did in the past and become better people *because* of it. You're working as an intern at the Foundation— you're doing good work. *That's* the part that counts."

She wasn't convinced. He could see it. "Okay, what did you do that was so bad?" he coaxed her. "Steal someone's boyfriend? Cheat on your college entrance exams? Drive a getaway car? Come on, Rachel, you have to get it off your chest so that you can start healing."

Rachel's head jerked up at the mention of the getaway car, stunned and a little indignant.

"No, I didn't drive a getaway car," she cried, horrified that he could even think something like that about her.

"See, that's my point exactly. You're not so bad," he told her, lightly caressing her face.

That was a matter of opinion, she thought. Looking back, she definitely didn't like the younger version of herself, the woman she had been five years ago.

"I was self-centered and petty and shallow," she told him.

He was *not* taken aback. "It's called being an adolescent," he told her.

"And that doesn't bother you, knowing that I was like that?"

Matteo laughed, thinking that she was adorable— and that, more likely than not, she was going to save him from becoming cynical and withdrawn.

"Nope. The only important thing is that you're none of those things now," he answered.

They had gone out on only a handful of dates. How could he possibly think he knew her well enough to say something so flattering about her character?

"How do you know that? What you just said, how do you *know* that I'm none of those things?" She wanted so badly for him to say something to convince her.

"I just do," he assured her. "I gave you a lot of excuses about why I wasn't there this morning when you woke up, why I ran. Everything I told you was true, but the main reason I pulled that vanishing act was because I was—" and this was still difficult for him to admit out loud, but it *was* the truth, so he had to tell her "—well, scared."

"Scared?" she repeated. She couldn't see Matteo Mendoza being afraid of anything. It just didn't seem to fit. "Of what?"

His mouth curved just a little. "Of you."

"Me?" She stared at Matteo as if he'd lost his mind. "Why would you possibly be scared of me?" For all he knew, she was a simple hostess, a fledgling intern, while he belonged to a big, loving family that backed him in any endeavor he set his mind to.

He'd started this, so it was up to him to see it through and tell her the truth. "Because of the way you made me feel. Because I knew that I loved you. That gave you power over me," he pointed out, "and I didn't want you to have that power."

"Power?" she repeated as if it was a foreign word. "What would I want with power over you?" He had to be pulling her leg, she thought. "You're not making any sense."

"What didn't make any sense was my running out on you this morning, and I'm really, really sorry about that. You're the best thing that ever happened to me." He anticipated her protest and headed it off by saying, "And I'm not just saying it because Cisco was interested in you. You knocked me for a total loop the first moment I saw you—and that was *before* Cisco had ever made a play for you."

Rachel regarded him skeptically. It went without saying that she was extremely attracted to him, really *felt* something for him—which was why she knew it would hurt once he returned to Miami or moved on to wherever he was going.

The possibility of his remaining with her never even crossed her mind. She was certain that when this interlude between them was over, she would be left behind. The very thought of Matteo going away without her once she'd opened her heart to him made her ache fiercely inside.

"I think you should know that I don't plan to give up," Matteo informed her. "I'm going to keep after you until I wear you down." There was a hint of mischief in his smile. "I just wanted to give you fair warning." His eyes were practically dancing as he added, "How does that old saying go? All's fair in love and war, right?"

He knew very well what that old saying was, she thought. He knew far too much for *her* own good.

"You're going to regret this," she warned him so solemnly, it gave him pause and had him wondering all over again about the nature of the deep, dark secret that was eating away at her.

But Rachel would tell him when she was ready. He was confident of that. In the meantime, he was going to avail himself of her company and focus on the positive aspects rather than search for the negative ones, the way he always used to do.

She had improved him already, Matteo realized with a smile. And she didn't even know it.

"The only thing I'm going to regret," he told her, "is if you suddenly take off and vanish from my life without a trace."

She looked at him, startled. He'd practically described to a T what she had done to her family five years ago. It had taken her a while to make herself get in touch with her mother. Even then, their contact had been short and abrupt. She'd let her mother know that she was fine and that she was trying to find herself without relying on the aid of family money.

It wasn't really the truth, at least not entirely. But this way, her mother didn't worry that she had been kidnapped or was lying dead at the bottom of some ditch. Her behavior could be written off as typically rebellious rather than something worse. In her case, a reaction to discovering that everything she had once thought to be true was really a lie. A lie perpetuated by the father she had once worshipped and adored.

"What?" Matteo asked in response to the look on her face. "Was that what you were planning?" he wanted to know, thinking he'd accidentally hit the nail on the head. "To vanish? It's not nearly as easy as it sounds—and I'd look for you," he told her. "I'd go to the ends of the earth to find you if I had to."

She was about to laugh that off, but something in his eyes kept her from doing that.

Rachel looked at him for a long moment. Amid the lighter banter was a solid vein of truth. "You mean that, don't you?" she asked. "You'd really come and look for me if I suddenly took off."

Matteo nodded. "Now you're getting the picture," he told her.

She was silent for a moment, thinking over what he'd just said and carefully examining how that made her feel. She would have expected it to make her feel hemmed in, maybe even trapped.

But it didn't.

It had a completely different effect. Matteo made her feel as if she mattered. As if he wanted to keep her safe and protected. It had been a long time since she had felt that way. It was a comforting feeling, knowing that there was someone who cared that much about her.

She supposed she owed him something for that, for making her feel as if she was part of something, part of some*one*.

So she gave him just a sliver of information.

"My father's estranged from his family."

She'd learned that much, at least, during her research into her father's true background. For some mysterious reason, it seemed that he had turned his back on his parents and siblings and on who he really was. That was when "Gerald Robinson" was born.

"That's too bad," Matteo told her, sounding as if he genuinely meant it. "According to my dad, one of his brothers is like that, won't talk to the rest of the family for some reason, most likely because of an imagined slight he thought he'd suffered. Nobody can even remember what it was about or how it all started.

"I have a whole bunch of cousins I've never gotten to know. It feels kind of strange, knowing there's a number of people who are my family, yet I wouldn't recognize them even if I tripped over them on the street," Matteo told her. There was genuine regret in his voice.

Rachel said nothing, offering neither a comment nor any sort of condolences. He knew that was his cue to leave the subject alone.

So he did.

For now, he was focused on making her feel safe with him. Feeling safe involved knowing that she could relax around him and not worry about being unexpectedly interrogated about something she had no desire to talk about.

Matteo changed the subject. "That was a great dinner," he told her.

The fact that he was saying it to her like a compliment made her laugh. After all, she hadn't had a hand in preparing it. She'd just put it into her car and carried it into her apartment.

"I unpacked it all with my own little hands," she quipped.

"Hey, unpacking is important. It has to be done just right," he deadpanned.

She broke down, laughing. It felt wonderful as the tension slipped away from her. "You're crazy, you know that, right?"

Matteo surprised her by stealing one small kiss, then saying, "Sure I'm crazy. Crazy about you." He nodded at the squadron of empty plates all over the kitchen table. "Let me help you with the dishes."

The last thing she had on her mind right now was dishes that needed washing. He'd just brushed his lips against hers, behaving exactly as if they were a couple, comfortable with one another and having done things like that— casually stealing kisses—for years now.

If only that could be a reality…

Would you still want to steal kisses from me if you knew who I was? Whose daughter I was? And that I'm keeping all that from you because I don't want to drive you away?

She didn't want to think about the answer.

Matteo ran the tips of his fingers along her forehead, lightly—but firmly—smoothing it out. She looked at him quizzically.

"You're doing too much thinking," he told her. "Your forehead is furrowing again. You're forcing me to take action."

"What sort of action?"

"To keep you smiling, of course," he told her as if it was the only logical course of action.

"And just how do you intend to do that?" Rachel asked.

In order to keep her hands busy—and off him— she had turned her attention to arranging the dishes behind one another in the dishwasher.

Matteo took the rest of the dishes out of her hands before she had a chance to line them up. He put them back on the counter, his attention completely focused on her.

"Oh, I think I can come up with something," he

told her just before he took her into his arms. And then he kissed her again.

She had every intention of resisting, of blocking out the sensations that she knew would jump to the fore the second she let her guard down.

But it was already too late.

The very moment his lips touched hers, they also touched off a series of explosions within her, explosions that broke apart all the walls she had fooled herself into believing she could resurrect and retain against the onslaught of passions and sensations that Matteo seemed to draw out of her just with his very presence.

She was melting in the very spot where she was standing.

Her arms went around his neck, holding him closer, melding her body against his so that she could feel every delicious eruption at its conception as well as following it to its ultimate release.

Suddenly, the hours between last night and now, with all their insecurities and recriminations, completely disappeared as if they had never even existed, burned away in the fire that was being created by the two of them as they came together.

All there was, was now and the glorious endeavor of lovemaking.

Rachel abandoned herself to it, living in the moment and loving it.

As well as loving him.

For once, just for now, all her excuses vanished, and all that remained was the truth.

Whether it was going to set her free or imprison her remained to be seen.

Chapter Fifteen

"So, have you given any more thought to returning to Miami, Matteo?" Orlando asked his son.

They were flying in another shipment to the Fortune Foundation's new office. This would be the last one before this branch's official grand opening.

The surrounding sky was a perfect blue, the kind that could make a man forget his mundane, day-to-day annoyances and problems and lose himself in the majesty of the heavens as he soared, unencumbered.

Flying in this sort of a setting also made a man look at the bigger picture. It always had for him, Orlando thought.

Orlando glanced now at his son in the copilot seat. Who would have ever thought that small, sensitive young boy would have grown into the man he now saw sitting next to him?

The years were going by much too quickly, Orlando thought. He needed to make the most of them while he was still able.

"You trying to get rid of me, Dad?" Matteo asked, obviously amused at his father's phrasing.

"You know better than that," Orlando told him. "I would like nothing better than to have you all stay right here in Horseback Hollow. Yes, I know it doesn't have the kind of nightlife Miami has, but as you get older, you realize that there are far more important things in life than partying until dawn."

"I know," Matteo replied quietly.

Considering how imperative Matteo had made nightlife sound only a few weeks ago, his simple affirmation now surprised Orlando.

"You do?"

"Yeah, I do," Matteo said. "I've been thinking that it's time I decided what I wanted to do with the rest of my life."

This was beginning to sound very hopeful, Orlando thought. "And what did you decide?"

Matteo turned in his seat, looking at his father. "Dad, how would you like a partner?"

By nature, Orlando had always been a cautious man who didn't count his chickens until he'd watched all of them hatch. He needed more input before he declared this to be a victory.

"What sort of a partner?" he wanted to know.

"At the Redmond Flight School and Charter Service—specifically at the Charter Service branch of it." Matteo supposed he was taking a lot for granted. Just because he'd been hovering around his father, elbowing his way onto every supply run his father had made back and forth between Red Rock and Horseback Hollow, didn't mean his father would be willing to accept his presence on a permanent basis.

"I'd like that fine, Matteo," Orlando told him, a smile covering his distinguished, handsome face. "Just let me run it by Sawyer and Laurel," he said, referring to the owners of the business. "Though I'm sure they'll be happy to have you."

"Good, because working with you will help me pay the mortgage on that ranch house I just put a deposit down on," Matteo deadpanned.

Orlando's mouth dropped open. "A ranch hou— When were you planning on telling me this?" he cried, stunned as well as delighted.

Matteo grinned broadly. "I just did."

"But I had to ask," Orlando pointed out.

"I just did it yesterday, Dad. I'm still getting used to the idea myself," Matteo told him. He nodded toward the controls. "If you're tired, I can take over, you know."

Orlando laughed, shaking his head. "Yes, I know, and I am not tired. You should know by now that flying makes me feel alive. It's good to have a passion," he pronounced with feeling. He slanted another glance toward his son. "Speaking of that, have you and that pretty girl with the two jobs resolved your problems yet?"

Rachel was the underlying reason why Matteo had decided to risk everything and change his entire life around. Considering that they hadn't even remotely discussed the future beyond one-week periods, he knew he was taking a huge chance.

No risk, no gain, right? he told himself.

Even though he's just shared some of his plans with his father, he wasn't altogether sure he wanted to discuss the romance aspect of his life just yet—beyond getting the older man to use her name rather than to refer to her as "girl."

"Rachel, Dad. Her name is Rachel."

Orlando nodded. "That's right, I forget. All right," he tried again, "have you and Rachel resolved your problems?"

Matteo still didn't feel he was up to discussing anything of such a personal nature just yet, at least not until he had some positive feedback from Rachel to work with.

"I really don't know what you're talking about, Dad."

On a roll, his father apparently couldn't be put off. "Of course you do. I did not raise any stupid children. Anyone can see that you care about this Rachel, and she certainly seems to light up whenever you are around. You want my opinion," he went on as if Matteo had just said yes.

"I think it's time for you to stop dragging your feet and do something about the way you feel." Orlando paused, then went a layer deeper. Who knew when another opportunity for a heart-to-heart with his youngest son would present itself? "This thing between you and your brother, it has to stop, you know."

Matteo *definitely* didn't want to talk about this. "Tell him, not me."

His father caught him off guard by saying, "I have. Cisco claims that he was only doing it for your own good."

"Jumping the gun and asking Rachel out before I

got the chance was for my own good?" That was a load of horse manure, and both his father and brother knew it, Matteo thought.

"According to Cisco, he feels that it was his behaving that way that finally got you to make a move. Otherwise," Orlando continued, "Cisco believes you would still be standing at the starting gate, hesitating to take even a single step forward."

Matteo resented being second-guessed, even by family—and especially by someone he thought of as being far too smug. "Oh, he did, did he?"

"Yes, he did. And to be perfectly honest, son, I believed him when he said he did that for you," Orlando confided. "I know that Cisco is perhaps a little unorthodox—"

"A *little*?" Matteo echoed in disbelief. "He's the poster boy for unorthodox, Dad," he insisted.

Orlando frowned. His son had just given him good news, but it was all for nothing if members of the family were feuding or not talking to one another at all. He needed to have this feud nipped in the bud, before it became too big to handle.

"Matteo, I want you to settle things with Cisco," he said seriously.

Matteo was honest with his father. "I don't know if I want to be bothered, Dad."

For a moment there was silence, and Matteo thought that his father had dropped the subject, at least for now. He should have known better.

"If you don't," Orlando said quietly, "if you allow this, this *thing* between you to grow and fester, you will wind up regretting it for the rest of your life."

He gave his younger son a penetrating look. "Trust me, I know."

The level of emotion in his father's voice surprised him. Matteo looked at his father, wanting to ask questions, to find out just what was behind those words, but he instinctively knew that this was a subject that couldn't be touched upon, at least not yet.

Not until his father was ready.

His father, he could tell, was also waiting for an affirmative response from him. For the sake of family peace, Matteo surrendered.

"I'll talk to him," Matteo promised, even though it cost him to do so.

"Good boy," Orlando responded with a broad smile.

Matteo had promised his father to make amends, and he had never intentionally broken his word to anyone, but this time, he was sorely tempted to do just that.

No matter how confident he felt, whatever strides he'd taken, the moment he was in Cisco's presence, all that progress seemed to vanish. He suddenly became the awkward kid brother standing in his older, more sophisticated brother's shadow.

But a promise was a promise. He knew he at least had to try.

So once he and his father had landed the small aircraft and unloaded it, putting the supplies onto Orlando's waiting truck, Matteo forced himself to make a side trip to Cisco's real-estate investment office. His brother had surprised all of them by making arrangements to set up the storefront office temporarily.

He'd told his father that he wanted to test the waters in Horseback Hollow before deciding to make the move permanent. Matteo had a feeling that Cisco had other reasons for setting up the office, but that was his brother's business, and he wasn't going to pry.

Right now, Matteo wanted to get this so-called peace talk over with as soon as possible. This was something he definitely did not want looming over his head. He was well aware that the disagreement would only grow into unmanageable proportions if he allowed any amount of time to pass.

Even so, Matteo stood outside his brother's door for a moment, looking in and wondering if it was too late to turn on his heel and go.

And then Cisco looked up from his desk and saw Matteo through the bay window. The door on his opportunity to escape slammed shut.

Resigned, Matteo walked in. "I guess you've decided to settle in Horseback Hollow," he said, gesturing around at the office.

"Never miss out on what could be an opportunity," Cisco responded, then asked, "So, to what do I owe this unexpected pleasure?"

Having Matteo appear on his doorstep had caught him totally off guard, but he was accustomed to recovering quickly. In less than half a minute, he had gotten himself together and acted as if this was a regular occurrence between them.

Because of the way Matteo viewed their relationship, every word out of Cisco's mouth always sounded as if it was dripping with sarcasm to him.

But he was here, so he might as well give this a decent shot. "Dad thinks we should call a truce."

"A truce?" Cisco repeated. "Is there a war going on between us?" he asked innocently. He gestured toward the chair next to his desk. "Why don't you have a seat?"

Matteo would have preferred to stand, but for the sake of appearing genial and moving this along, he sat down in the only other chair in the room besides Cisco's. He sat on the edge as if ready to take flight at less than a moment's notice.

"You know there's a war," Matteo said pointedly.

Still maintaining an innocent expression, Cisco looked at him and asked in the same tone, "Are you at war with me, Matteo?"

Did he really think he could use this act to his advantage? "Actually, it's more like the other way around," he told Cisco. "You're the one who's at war with me."

"No, I'm not," Cisco told him. "I think I'd know it if I were."

Why was Cisco denying it? They both knew what Matteo said was true. "What do you call undermining me at every turn?"

"I call it lighting a fire under you—and it's not at every turn, just the ones I think are important," Cisco corrected his brother.

Did Cisco expect Matteo to be grateful for this? His brother had just admitted to manipulating him like some mindless marionette.

"So now you're a master puppeteer who's pulling the strings? And I'm what, your puppet?" Matteo demanded. The very thought of that was an insult to him.

The next moment, he told himself that meeting

Cisco like this to hash it out had been a bad idea. Better to let sleeping dogs lie indefinitely than to poke them with a stick.

For his part, Cisco appeared to take offense at what was being said, as well.

"No, you're my thick-headed little—excuse me— younger brother," he corrected himself, "who moves around like he's got glue in his veins and uses me as an excuse *not* to act on his feelings. All I did was goad you a little. Hell, Mattie, you and Rachel belong together. If I could see it, so could you. I figured if I acted as if I were interested in her, you'd wake up and snap to it instead of letting that girl slip through your fingers."

Matteo's head was spinning. Right about now, black was white and down was up. "So you're not interested in her?"

Cisco leaned back in his chair. "I'm interested in *every* woman, but not in a permanent way. If this one has caught your fancy, then you have my blessings. Enjoy." Cisco grinned knowingly. "If my instincts serve me correctly, you already have enjoyed her, haven't you?"

He held up his hand before Matteo could say something sarcastic in response.

"That was a rhetorical question. That wasn't poking around for an answer or any details," he assured Matteo. Pausing, he grew serious and asked, "It *is* serious between you two, isn't it?"

Matteo shrugged his broad shoulders. He still had to work a few kinks out. "I'm not sure."

Cisco shook his head. His brother was making this

way more complicated than it actually was. "You either care about the lady, or you don't," Cisco told him.

That was the only part Matteo was sure of. "Oh, I care about her, all right. I care about Rachel a great deal."

Cisco spread his hands, confounded. "So what's the problem?"

Matteo sighed, looking off into space. "It's complicated."

Cisco was not buying that. His brother was just using another excuse. "Only as complicated as you make it," Cisco told him.

Because this actually was beginning to have the makings of a truce, Matteo leveled with his brother. "I've got some misgivings."

"About her?" Cisco asked.

"In a way—yes, about her," Matteo said, changing his mind midsentence about just how far he wanted to take this.

Cisco looked genuinely interested. Ordinarily, he would have thought it was an act, but now he wasn't sure. "What kind of misgivings?" he asked.

Matteo told him what had been eating away at him almost from the start, when he'd asked Rachel about her family. "I don't think she's being entirely honest with me."

"About what?" Cisco prodded him.

"There's something about her family that she's not being entirely honest about."

That, to Cisco, was small potatoes. Definitely *not* something to cause a breakup in a promising relationship. And from what he'd picked up, Matteo and Rachel had all the makings of a promising relationship.

"Hey, little brother, Rachel's human. Everyone is entitled to have *some* secrets. Secrets keep you on your toes and make a person more interesting, if you ask me." He smiled as he said, "Oh, ye who are without secrets, cast the first stone."

Matteo frowned. "I don't want to cast the first stone—or any stone. I just want to feel that she trusts me and knows she can confide in me."

"Time, buddy," Cisco advised him. "That kind of thing takes time. But you and the lady will get there—just take it one step at a time. Show her that she can count on you not just when you want to be there but when she *needs* you to be there, as well."

It suddenly hit Matteo that Cisco was giving him some very solid, sage pieces of advice. "Where are you coming up with all this?"

"On-the-job training, Mattie. On-the-job training. Now, go and make me proud," Cisco urged him with a fond wink. "Oh, and I get dibs on being best man once you and she get around to tying the knot."

Matteo formed a fist and knocked on his brother's desk twice, as if to counteract a jinx. "If we ever finally do get to that point," he told Cisco, "the job's yours."

Cisco laughed. "I'll hold you to that."

Matteo had absolutely no doubt that his brother would do just that. And when it came right down to it, if this *did* turn out the way he hoped it would, then he definitely *wanted* Cisco as his best man.

But first Rachel had to say yes.

Rachel didn't know why she should have these butterflies crashing into one another inside her stomach.

After all, she wasn't going to be called upon to speak. Her boss, Christopher Fortune Jones, was. Her only function here was to be one of the well-wishers and enjoy the ribbon-cutting ceremony.

A substantial number of people had responded to the invitation to attend the ceremony. They gathered in front of the brand-new building that housed the latest branch of the Fortune Foundation.

In addition to all the people who would be working at the Foundation, the ceremony was being attended by some of the more important members of the Fortune family. There was Emmett Jamison, the former FBI agent who ran the Foundation these days, Lily Fortune, still a stunning, exotic-looking woman at sixty-nine, and James Marshall Fortune. James was the sixty-three-year-old family member who, Rachel had heard, had gone through such great pains to find his two sisters—he was one of a set of triplets and the only member of the family to have been kept as a Fortune, while the other two had been given up for adoption.

It was because of James's relentless efforts that Christopher's mother finally found out about her true identity.

Rachel looked at the faces around her, faces that belonged to members of the Fortune family.

Look at them all, she thought.

She didn't know why she felt such butterflies dive-bombing inside her. Was it anxiety causing this reaction?

Or something else?

A hush fell over the crowd as Christopher stepped forward. Wielding a giant set of scissors, the newly minted member of the Fortune family cut the ribbon in front of the building, signaling the official opening of the Fortune Foundation.

Once both sides of the wide red ribbon had gently floated to the ground, cries of "Speech" echoed throughout the crowd. Resigned, Christopher put down the scissors and reluctantly gave the onlookers what they asked for.

"I don't really have a speech," he confessed. "I'm not much good at talking to more than a couple of people at a time. But I just wanted to say that I still wake up in the morning and think that all this was just a dream. That James Marshall Fortune did not come into my life and the lives of my siblings and mother, and he didn't tell us that we were all part of the Fortune family—long-lost members he had finally tracked down.

"As you all probably know, I resisted at first, as did some other members of my immediate family, because we had the misconception that the Fortune family was made up of snobs who thought of themselves as being privileged. Boy, was I wrong."

Laughter met his statement, and he waited until it died down before continuing.

"I can't tell you exactly what it means to find out that you're a Fortune—I'm still learning about that part every day. But I can tell you that it comes with a warm feeling, knowing there's a network of people who have your back. A network of people you can always turn to if there's a problem.

"Being a Fortune means never, ever being alone, even if you think you are. I had to learn that the hard way because I resisted taking on the name, resisted the idea that I was part of them and they were part of me. But I'm not always bright about things. I do know, thanks to them, that you can never have too much family. Until my dying day, I will always be grateful that Uncle James has embraced all the Fortunes of Horseback Hollow. You have no idea what that means to all of us, Uncle James."

He addressed these last words to the man who had brought about this vast change in his life.

James nodded in response, a smile gracing his thin lips.

A wave of applause went up.

Rachel had tried, really tried, to stand there and smile as her boss talked about this rare gift that had been bestowed on him and on the members of his family. She'd almost made it through the entire speech intact, her eyes dry, her body almost rigid. She was determined that no one around her would guess the secret that she had been living with for the past five years.

But when Christopher continued to go on about what it meant to be a Fortune, and then turned toward James Marshall Fortune to sincerely thank him for embracing *all* the Fortunes—while she was standing out here in the cold, unrecognized and certainly not part of the actual inner circle, something within Rachel just gave way.

The dam broke. Before she could stop herself, she was crying. Tears were sliding down her cheeks. At any second, one of the Foundation's guests would notice and could very well start asking all manner of questions.

Questions she didn't trust herself to answer coherently right now. Feeling like an outcast, she was far too emotional to deal with something like that properly.

Rachel bolted, blindly running from the area and praying that she would be able to find someplace to hide until she could cry this out of her system.

Barring that, she'd just go home. She had made a grave mistake coming to the ceremony.

She didn't belong here.

Rachel was beginning to feel that she didn't really belong anywhere.

Chapter Sixteen

At the last minute, Matteo had come, along with his father, his sister, Gabi, and her new husband, Jude Fortune Jones, to take part in the dedication ceremony. Truthfully, he was paying far less attention than he should have to what Christopher was saying. Instead, he was busy searching the crowd for Rachel.

Which was why he saw her when she ran from the gathering. Surprised, he was quick to follow.

Within moments, it became obvious to him that Rachel's long legs were not just for show. She covered an impressive amount of ground in a short time.

He was really having trouble catching up to her. She zigzagged through the crowd, making a beeline for the perimeter. He had no idea where she was heading after that.

All he knew was that he had to catch her before

she disappeared on him. He'd caught a glimpse of her face from a distance and saw that she was crying.

He couldn't even begin to guess why.

But something was very wrong. He needed to get to the bottom of this, to make it right no matter what it took.

For the first time since they had initially gotten together, he realized that Rachel had the makings of a prize-winning runner.

If he was going to catch her, Matteo told himself, he was going to have to dig deep and really pour it on.

So he did.

Rachel didn't realize that anyone was running after her until she was more than half a block away from the Fortune Foundation building. The sound of rhythmic footfalls directly behind her registered in her brain. The sound was getting closer.

And then someone was catching her arm and pulling her around to face him.

Her heart thudded against her rib cage.

Matteo.

"Rachel, what's wrong?" Matteo asked, almost undone by the sight of her tears. Every protective fiber of his being went on red alert. "You're shaking. And you're crying," he said needlessly. "Why are you crying?"

She didn't want to talk about it. She couldn't. He'd think she was being an idiot. But that still didn't take the pain away. "Dedication speeches always make me sad."

"Okay, you got that out of your system," he said, pushing the quip aside. "Now tell me the truth." He put a hand on each of her shoulders, just in case she was thinking of darting away again. "What happened back there to make you cry? What's wrong?"

But Rachel just shrugged, wishing he would drop the subject. "It's complicated."

He hadn't thought it was going to be a simple matter. "That's all right. I have all afternoon. And if that's not enough time, I can clear the rest of the evening, as well." He had no intention of leaving her side until she told him everything. She was in no condition to be left alone.

Rachel waved him away. "You won't understand," she told him.

But Matteo remained steadfast. His place was here, with her, even if she didn't know it yet. "Then *make* me understand," he told her. "Why are you crying?" he repeated patiently.

Matteo was not going to leave until she told him. She could see that in the set of his chin, the look in his eyes. He had a very sensitive, sensual face, but it could also be an exceedingly stubborn face, as well.

So she proceeded to tell him—and braced herself for either ridicule or annoyed dismissal.

"Because Christopher was going on about how James Fortune was embracing the missing branch of the family he'd discovered in Horseback Hollow and how wonderful everything was going to be."

Matteo still didn't see a reason for her to burst into tears. "What about that—other than being maybe a little bit syrupy?"

She avoided his eyes and looked at the ground as she said, "It's not true."

Matteo was doing his best to understand what

she was telling him and why she was so upset, but it wasn't easy. She was giving him middle pieces of the jigsaw puzzle without allowing him to see any of the defining corners.

"Then he's not embracing them?" Matteo asked, using the word she had repeated, since it seemed somehow important to the underlying matter.

"No, not all of them," Rachel told him, still avoiding his eyes.

Matteo hadn't heard anything about the patriarch turning his back on anyone, as she seemed to be telling him, but he refrained from saying as much to Rachel.

Instead, he asked, "Who's James rejecting?" When she finally raised her face to look at him, there was something there in her eyes, something she'd been hiding. A glimmer that suddenly flashed the answer to him. "You?" he asked her uncertainly.

The moment he asked, he knew.

It *was* her.

But how was that possible? She'd said her last name was Robinson. As far as he knew, that wasn't a surname associated with the Fortunes.

Had Rachel been lying to him all along? Was her last name really Fortune? But what reason would she have to hide that?

Try as he might, he just couldn't see her doing that. He would have bet any amount of money that Rachel *couldn't* lie. Lying just wasn't part of her makeup.

There was no point in hiding it anymore, Rachel thought. The other Fortunes, new or otherwise, wouldn't accept her as one of them, so making herself publicly known as a Fortune served no purpose there.

But it did here, between Matteo and her. She wasn't about to lie to him, the man she loved, even if part of her was afraid he'd turn his back on her because she'd kept this from him until now.

"Yes," she told him stoically, "I'm a Fortune—at least, I think so."

He had to admit, this nearly knocked him for a loop. "How do you know that?" he asked. "Wait, start from the beginning."

Taking her hand, he led her even farther away from the Fortune Foundation building. He was playing a hunch that if she went on a walk with him, talking might come more easily for her.

"The beginning," she repeated, as if to orient herself where that would be. "Okay. I grew up thinking that my father, Gerald Robinson, was this computer genius who started up his own company and made a ton of money while he was at it. He wasn't around all that much, and I thought it was his work that kept him away. Other kids' fathers were workaholics, so it was okay that mine was, too.

"Dad tried to make up for his absences by giving my brothers and sisters—and me—everything we could possibly have wanted. Private lessons in everything imaginable, expensive clothes." She paused for a moment as the irony of what she was about to say next got to her. "Whatever we wanted, we got. I realize now that he did that to make up for his guilty conscience—not because he was away from us, working, but because he was away from us…indulging in other things," she finally said as delicately as possible.

"Other things?" Matteo repeated. He wasn't sure he understood what she meant.

It took her a second to make peace with what she was about to share—and then she told him.

"Women. I think he was trying to fill some inner void. My dad was—and most likely still is—estranged from his family. I don't know why or how it started, but I got the feeling that they were the ones who turned their backs on him—although maybe it was the other way around. I don't know for sure. All I do know is that I feel like I've been living a lie all of my life."

"You're not the one who's lived a lie, Rachel. Your father's the one who did. He's the one who lied to you, not the other way around." Matteo could understand why she felt so disoriented, so rejected, and he didn't want her going through this alone. He was there with her all the way, starting from this moment on. "And you think that your father's really a Fortune?"

She nodded. "Just before I finally left home, I looked through some of his things —he was away again, as usual, and my mother was gone with some of her friends for the weekend. I found some correspondence addressed to a Jerome Fortune and a very old driver's license for the same name. The picture on it belonged to a much younger version of my father." She remembered that her heart had stopped when she saw the picture. At that moment, it was as if her life had literally turned on its head. "He's either got a dead ringer wandering around somewhere with his face—or my father is one of the Fortunes."

He still didn't see the problem. It could be so easily resolved, in his estimation. "If that's what you think, why haven't you said something to one of them? You see Christopher several times a week. You could have told him your suspicions. He might have helped you find out the truth one way or another."

She shook her head. The fewer people in on this secret, the better. "If I'm right, they didn't want my father. Why would they want me?"

"Are you kidding?" Matteo cried, stunned by her question. He stopped walking and turned to look at her. "I can't imagine anyone *not* wanting you." He gently pushed aside a few stray hairs from her face, lightly caressing her cheek. "I want you every minute of every day. I want you so badly, I can *taste* it."

Rachel found that she was having trouble swallowing. "You're just saying that," she whispered hoarsely, her eyes never leaving his.

"I'm *just saying* that because it's true," he told her. "I meant what I said the other day, Rachel. I'm in love with you, and I want to be with you. Forever. If you'll have me," he qualified. He didn't want her feeling that she had no choice in the matter—although it would kill him if she didn't want to be with him.

"Stop talking like that," she warned him. "Or you'll make me say yes."

"That's the whole idea," he pointed out.

There was a time when she'd bought into happily-ever-after, but now she wouldn't dare. There were too many obstacles in the way. She didn't want to believe him and then go on to have all her hopes dashed because he had come to his senses.

"You don't know what you're saying," she told him. "Besides, you're going back to Miami soon."

Once again, he surprised her by telling her, "No, I'm not."

Then he was staying here? With her? "Don't do

this, Matteo. Don't tease me like this." She didn't want to deal with more disappointment. She'd had enough to last a lifetime.

"If I was planning to go back to Miami, why did I put money down on a ranch house right here in Horse-back Hollow?" he asked her innocently.

This was the first she'd heard of it. He hadn't even mentioned that he was *thinking* about buying a ranch house.

"You did what?" she asked, stunned.

"I bought a house." But he had more news than that to share with her. "And I'm going to be working with my dad at the Redmond Flight School and Charter Service." He grinned. He and his father had had a few rocky moments as well as differences of opinion on some matters, but now everything was stabilizing, and he had every reason to think things would continue on this even keel. "We've worked out the details."

"But what about the nightlife in Miami?" she asked, remembering that he had told her there was nothing like it and that he couldn't wait to get back to it. "You said you missed it."

"Not half as much as I'd miss you if I left," he told her with all sincerity.

He knew without asking that this was where she wanted to be. He might convince her to come with him to Miami, but she wouldn't be happy there. Besides, Horseback Hollow was growing on him, God help him.

"Miami nightlife will have to go on without me." He smiled at her. "I found something much better to do with my time—convincing you to be my wife. If you'll have me."

"Matteo—" she began.

He couldn't read her expression, which meant that he didn't know what she was going to say.

What he was afraid of was that she was going to turn him down, saying no to his proposal. Right now, he couldn't face hearing that hurtful word, so he began to talk quickly, hoping to steer Rachel's conversation in a slightly different direction.

"I want you to know I'm not going to pressure you," he told her solemnly. "You can take as long as you like to make up your mind."

Rachel tried again. "Matteo—"

And again he headed her off. "You don't have to give me an answer anytime soon, Rachel. Really. I'm good. I can wait as long as I have to in order to hear you give me the right answer."

"Matteo—" There was just a little bit of an edge to her voice this time.

"I'm serious," he continued, talking right over her. "You don't have to say anything now. We can go back to the ceremony like nothing's happened and—"

"Matteo!" Frustrated at not being able to squeeze in a single word, even edgewise, Rachel finally raised her voice to almost a shout so that it would be heard over his voice.

"What?" Matteo asked, fearing that defeat was tottering just an inch away.

He knew that she certainly hadn't had enough time to think this through yet. He needed time to convince her about this.

"Yes!" Rachel finally declared the second there was an iota of silence between them.

For a second, the word didn't register with Matteo, shimmering instead just on the outskirts of his comprehension. And then it hit him what she was saying yes to.

Or at least what he fervently *hoped* she was saying yes to.

"Yes?" he asked, almost hesitantly, watching her face intently.

This time Rachel nodded as well, her smile so wide, he thought he could just fall into it and stay basking in the wattage for a couple of lifetimes, all his needs met and answered.

"Yes," she assured him.

He had to be sure, crystal clear sure. "Do you mean yes, you'll marry me?"

"Of course I mean yes, I'll marry you—if you're absolutely sure you want me." Rachel still felt she had to qualify her words—just in case.

For his part, Matteo looked almost serene when he answered, "I have never been so sure of anything in my life."

"Then what are you waiting for?" she asked, clearly expecting something. "Aren't proposals usually sealed with a kiss?"

"You're right," he said solemnly. He was able to maintain that look for a total of five seconds before the smile came out. "What was I thinking?"

"That you want to kiss me, I hope," Rachel told him in a low, sultry voice that was meant for moments just like this.

He left nothing more up in the air, or to chance. Neither did he allow another second to go by without kissing the woman who had simultaneously conquered him and crowned him emperor of his world, of *their* world, all with the same breath.

"I have no idea what I did," he said, enfolding her in his arms, "to deserve this. To deserve you."

"Santa said you were a very, very good boy this year," she teased him.

"Remind me to give Santa a discount shipping rate for his annual run this year," he told her.

"Consider it done," she murmured just a second before her lips found his. "No more talking," she told him. "Just doing."

"No more talking," he agreed.

And, as always, Matteo Mendoza was a man of his word.

Epilogue

Battling the sweetest kind of exhaustion that a man could ever wish for, Matteo fell back on the king-size hotel bed in the throes of waning euphoria. With his last bit of strength, he threaded his arm around the woman who had so quickly become the center of his universe and drew her even closer to him.

"Wow," he gasped when he could finally suck in enough air to form words. "You've completely worn me out, woman. You keep that up and I'm not going to live long enough to make it to the wedding."

Grinning, Rachel turned her body into his, glorying in his sensual warmth.

"I'm afraid you brought that on yourself by being such a stud. But if you're having trouble keeping up, we could always postpone the wedding. That way, you can build up your strength."

"Postpone the wedding?" he echoed. "And risk you changing your mind? Not on your life." Running the back of his hand along her cheek, Matteo grew a little more serious. "How did I get to be so lucky?" he asked in a whisper.

Rachel's eyes crinkled. "Funny, I was just thinking the same thing."

"Now all I need is an unlimited supply of vitamins to keep up with you, and I'm all set." He tightened his arm around Rachel just a little more. "Tell me, what do you think about the summer?" he wanted to know.

Rachel pretended to think over his question seriously. "It's usually a little hotter, but in general, it's a nice season."

He laughed and shook his head. She was one of a kind, and he adored her. "I meant for the wedding, wise guy."

"Spring, summer, fall, today, tomorrow night, whenever you want to do it is fine with me." The important thing was that he loved her. Everything else was a distant second.

"We're going to need some time to get everything ready," he pointed out, nibbling a little on her shoulder. The woman had the sexiest limbs he'd ever come across. Everything about her just drove him wild.

"I'm ready at any time," she responded.

Any time did not leave time for all the trappings that went with a wedding. "The words *wedding gown*, *wedding cake*, *wedding invitations*, *reception hall* mean anything to you?" he wanted to know.

"Yes, headaches. They mean headaches," she underscored. "I don't need all that as long as I have you." And she meant that from the bottom of her heart. He was all she required for her happily-ever-after.

Matteo looked at her in amazed disbelief. "I thought it was always the woman who wanted something big and fancy."

She spread one hand, indicating herself. "You got the exception."

"So did you, I'm afraid," he countered. He liked the idea of a big wedding, of showing Rachel off to the entire universe. "My father is very traditional. He likes to see his kids get married with all the trimmings." Matteo paused for a moment, studying her expression. And then it came to him. "You're worried about inviting your family, aren't you?"

Rachel shrugged one shoulder in halfhearted semi denial. "Not worried, exactly, but it's been five years since I've seen any of them." What if they all turned down the invitation? She tried to tell herself it wouldn't matter—but it would.

"Don't you think it's about time to put that all behind you, start fresh?" Matteo suggested. "Clean slate and all that stuff?"

"Is that why you insisted on bringing me here to Austin?" She'd wondered about that ever since he'd told her that he'd booked a suite at the Hilton Hotel right outside Austin. Wondered and worried, as well.

"I brought you here because this is the best hotel I know of. The fact that it's located in Austin is just a coincidence. Not that I mind. Coming here lets me see the city that's responsible for raising a beauty like you." He felt as if her eyes were boring straight into him. "Why are you staring at me like that?"

"I'm waiting for your nose to grow," Rachel said with a perfectly straight face.

His expression, on the other hand, was seductively wicked. "I'm lying here naked next to you," he pointed out. "That's not the part of me that's being affected."

She laughed and kissed him, then raised herself up on her elbow so she could get a better look at his face. "I'm being serious."

"So am I," he said, cupping the back of her head and bringing her mouth down to his.

"I can't say no to you when you do that," she told him, her words escaping on a breathless sigh.

"Lucky me," he murmured just before he began making love with her again.

Bemused, so in love she could hardly stand it, Rachel feigned being asleep and watched her fiancé head to the shower through barely opened eyes.

Matteo hadn't bothered putting anything on as he left the bed. For the hundredth time, she thought to herself that he had a truly magnificent body, the kind that created goose bumps in its wake.

She was very, very happy and luckier than she'd ever thought possible.

The bathroom door closed. She heard the sound of water being turned on. She was tempted to get up and surprise Matteo by joining him in the shower.

But first she had something else to do.

Though he hadn't said it in so many words, she knew that Matteo had brought her back to the city where she had grown up for a reason. He wanted her to make peace with her father, to reconcile their differences because he felt that she wouldn't have any peace until she did.

He knew her so well, Rachel thought now, smiling as she pulled the blanket over her.

Drawing the hotel phone over to her on the bed, she pressed a series of keys on the keypad. She surprised herself as her father's cell-phone number came back to her so easily.

The pit of her stomach quivered a little as she heard the phone on the other end ring. It tightened into a complete knot when she heard the deep male voice say "Hello?"

"Daddy? Daddy, it's Rachel," she said. "I'm here in Austin. Can I come by the house? I need to talk to you." Rachel paused for a second, then added, "It's about the Fortunes."

* * * * *

Don't miss the next chapter in

THE FORTUNES OF TEXAS: COWBOY COUNTRY

Cisco Mendoza is used to getting what he wants—by any means necessary. But when a lucrative job assignment puts him at odds with innocent Delaney Fortune, he has to choose between money—and love. Can Cisco find a way to have it all?

Look for
THE TAMING OF DELANEY FORTUNE
by Michelle Major

On sale April 2015, wherever Harlequin books and ebooks are sold.

COMING NEXT MONTH FROM

H **HARLEQUIN®**

SPECIAL EDITION

Available March 17, 2015

#2395 THE TAMING OF DELANEY FORTUNE
The Fortunes of Texas: Cowboy Country • by Michelle Major
Francisco Mendoza is having a bout of bad Fortune. Though he's been hired to help with the new Cowboy Country theme park, Cisco is told to lasso a member of the famous Fortune clan to help him out. So he courts spunky rancher Delaney Fortune Jones under the guise of helping him with his project...but falls for her instead! Can Delaney and Cisco find love in their very own pastures?

#2396 A DECENT PROPOSAL
The Bachelors of Blackwater Lake • by Teresa Southwick
When billionaire Burke Holden enters McKnight Automotive, he gets more than just an oil change. When beautiful mechanic Sydney McKnight asks him to be her pretend boyfriend, the sexy single dad happily accepts. But no-strings-attached can't last forever, especially since Burke's vowed to stay commitment-free. It might just take a true Montana miracle to give the Big Sky bachelor and the brunette beauty their very own happily-ever-after.

#2397 MEANT-TO-BE MOM
Jersey Boys • by Karen Templeton
Cole Rayburn's back home in Maple River, New Jersey...but he's definitely not a kid anymore. For one, he's got sole custody of his *own* two children; second, his boyhood best friend, Sabrina Noble, is all grown-up and easy on the eyes. Sabrina has just called off a disastrous engagement, so she's not looking to get buddy-buddy with any man...but it's soon clear that her bond with Cole is still very much alive. And he's not planning on letting her go—ever!

#2398 THE CEO'S BABY SURPRISE
The Prestons of Crystal Point • by Helen Lacey
Daniel Anderson is the richest and most arrogant man in town. He's also the most charming, and Mary-Jayne Preston falls under his spell—for one night. But that's all it takes for Mary-Jayne to fall pregnant with twins! The devastatingly handsome Daniel isn't daddy material, or so she thinks. As the mogul and the mom-to-be grow closer, can Daniel overcome his own tragic past to create a bright future with Mary-Jayne and their twins?

#2399 HIS SECRET SON
The Pirelli Brothers • by Stacy Connelly
Ten years ago, one night changed Lindsay Brookes's life forever, giving her a beloved son. But it didn't seem to mean as much to Ryder Kincaid, who went back to his cheerleader girlfriend. Now Lindsay is back home in Clearville, California, to tell her long-ago fling that he's a father. Already brokenhearted from a bitter divorce, Ryder is flabbergasted at this change of fortune...but little Trevor could bring together the family he's always dreamed of.

#2400 OH, BABY
The Crandall Lake Chronicles • by Patricia Kay
Sophie Marlowe and Dillon Burke parted ways long ago, but Fate has reunited the long-lost lovers. Sophie's young half sister and Dillon's nephew are expecting a baby, and it's up to these exes to help the youngsters create a happy family. Though the rakish former football player and the responsible guidance counselor seem to be complete opposites, there's no denying the irresistible attraction between them... and where there's smoke, there are flames of true love!

YOU CAN FIND MORE INFORMATION ON UPCOMING HARLEQUIN® TITLES, FREE EXCERPTS AND MORE AT WWW.HARLEQUIN.COM.

HSECNM0315

REQUEST YOUR FREE BOOKS!
2 FREE NOVELS PLUS 2 FREE GIFTS!

⬤ HARLEQUIN®

SPECIAL EDITION
Life, Love & Family

YES! Please send me 2 FREE Harlequin® Special Edition novels and my 2 FREE gifts (gifts are worth about $10). After receiving them, if I don't wish to receive any more books, I can return the shipping statement marked "cancel." If I don't cancel, I will receive 6 brand-new novels every month and be billed just $4.74 per book in the U.S. or $5.24 per book in Canada. That's a savings of at least 14% off the cover price! It's quite a bargain! Shipping and handling is just 50¢ per book in the U.S. and 75¢ per book in Canada.* I understand that accepting the 2 free books and gifts places me under no obligation to buy anything. I can always return a shipment and cancel at any time. Even if I never buy another book, the two free books and gifts are mine to keep forever.

235/335 HDN F45Y

Name _____ (PLEASE PRINT)

Address _____ Apt. #

City _____ State/Prov. _____ Zip/Postal Code

Signature (if under 18, a parent or guardian must sign)

Mail to the **Harlequin® Reader Service:**
IN U.S.A.: P.O. Box 1867, Buffalo, NY 14240-1867
IN CANADA: P.O. Box 609, Fort Erie, Ontario L2A 5X3

Want to try two free books from another line?
Call 1-800-873-8635 or visit www.ReaderService.com.

* Terms and prices subject to change without notice. Prices do not include applicable taxes. Sales tax applicable in N.Y. Canadian residents will be charged applicable taxes. Offer not valid in Quebec. This offer is limited to one order per household. Not valid for current subscribers to Harlequin Special Edition books. All orders subject to credit approval. Credit or debit balances in a customer's account(s) may be offset by any other outstanding balance owed by or to the customer. Please allow 4 to 6 weeks for delivery. Offer available while quantities last.

Your Privacy—The Harlequin® Reader Service is committed to protecting your privacy. Our Privacy Policy is available online at www.ReaderService.com or upon request from the Harlequin Reader Service.

We make a portion of our mailing list available to reputable third parties that offer products we believe may interest you. If you prefer that we not exchange your name with third parties, or if you wish to clarify or modify your communication preferences, please visit us at www.ReaderService.com/consumerschoice or write to us at Harlequin Reader Service Preference Service, P.O. Box 9062, Buffalo, NY 14269. Include your complete name and address.

HSE13R

"I don't know why you're willing to go along with this but
I'm grateful. Seriously, thanks."

"You're welcome."

Oddly enough it had been an easy decision. The simple
answer was that he'd agreed because she had asked and he
wanted to see her again. Granted, he could have asked her
out, but he'd already have had a black mark against him
because of turning down her request. Now she owed him.

Sydney leaned against the bar, a thoughtful look on her
face. "I've never done anything like this before, but I know
my father. He'll ask questions. In fact he already did. We're
going to need a cover story. How we met. How long we've
been dating. That sort of thing."

"It makes sense to be prepared."

"So we should get together soon and discuss it."

"What about right now?" Burke suggested.

Her eyes widened. "You don't waste time, do you?"

"No time like the present. Have you already had dinner?"

She shook her head. "Why?"

"Do you have a date?" If not, there was a very real possibility that she'd changed into the red blazer, skinny jeans and heels just for him. Probably wanted to look her best while making her case. Still, he really hoped she wasn't meeting another guy.

She gave him an ironic look. "Seriously? If I was going out with someone, I wouldn't have asked you to participate in this crazy scheme."

"Crazy? I don't know, it's a decent proposal." He shrugged. "So you're free. Have dinner with me. What about the restaurant here at the lodge? It's pretty good."

"The best in town." But she shook her head. "Too intimate."

So she didn't want to be alone with him. "Oh?"

"Something more public. People should see us together." She snapped her fingers. "The Grizzly Bear Diner would be perfect."

"I know the place. Both charming. And romantic."

"You're either being a smart-ass or a snob."

"Heaven forbid."

"You haven't been there yet?" she asked.

"No, I have."

He signaled the bartender, and when she handed the bill to him, he took care of it. Then he settled his hand at the small of her back and said, "Let the adventure begin."

Don't miss
A DECENT PROPOSAL
by Teresa Southwick,
available April 2015 wherever
Harlequin® Special Edition books and ebooks are sold.

www.Harlequin.com

HARLEQUIN®

A *Romance* FOR EVERY MOOD™

JUST CAN'T GET ENOUGH?

Join our social communities
and talk to us online.

You will have access to the latest
news on upcoming titles and special
promotions, but most importantly,
you can talk to other fans about your
favorite Harlequin reads.

Harlequin.com/Community

 Facebook.com/HarlequinBooks

Twitter.com/HarlequinBooks

Pinterest.com/HarlequinBooks